No one writes romantic fiction like Barbara Cartland.

Miss Cartland was originally inspired by the best of the romantic novelists she read as a girl —writers such as Elinor Glyn, Ethel M. Dell and E. M. Hull. Convinced that her own wide audience would also delight in her favorite authors, Barbara Cartland has taken their classic tales of romance and specially adapted them for today's readers.

Bantam is proud to publish these novels—personally selected and edited by Miss Cartland— under the imprint

**BARBARA CARTLAND'S
LIBRARY OF LOVE**

Bantam Books by Barbara Cartland
Ask your bookseller for the books you have missed

Barbara Cartland's Library of Love

Barbara Cartland's Library of Love

SIX DAYS
BY ELINOR GLYN
CONDENSED BY
BARBARA CARTLAND

BANTAM BOOKS
TORONTO · NEW YORK · LONDON

SIX DAYS
A Bantam Book | January 1978

ISBN 0–553–11376–3

Published simultaneously in the United States and Canada

Bantam Books are published by Bantam Books, Inc. Its trade-
mark, consisting of the words "Bantam Books" and the por-
trayal of a bantam, is registered in the United States Patent
Office and in other countries. Marca Registrada. Bantam
Books, Inc., 666 Fifth Avenue, New York, New York 10019.

PRINTED IN THE UNITED STATES OF AMERICA

Preface
by
Barbara Cartland

This entrancing love-story by Elinor Glyn develops the theme of true self-sacrificing love in a way which is irresistible.

No-one could be a more alluring heroine than Laline, and the skill with which the author unfolds her character and personality shows us how knowledgeable Elinor Glyn was about the human mind.

If what happened in the dug-out seems exaggerated to a modern generation, it is in fact perfectly possible that such a situation could arise.

I, myself, visited the battlefields in 1923 to see where my father had fought and died, and Elinor Glyn's descriptions bring back vididly the horror, the devastation, and the atmosphere of death which hung over the Flanders fields.

But love that is real is all-conquering and sweeps away the unsureness of everything but an ecstatic happiness.

Chapter
One
1921

David Lamont left the Minister's Cabinet with his spirit highly exalted.

What he had received instructions to do was going to be difficult, and the inference that he had been chosen out of the number that the Ministers could have selected from gave him satisfaction.

The President had been in the room for part of the time, and they had spoken softly and gravely, and one sentence would stay in David's memory to the day of his death:

"You have read the *Message to Garcia,* of course, Major Lamont; let it be your guide upon this difficult mission."

His mother had given him the little booklet when it had first appeared in America, after the Cuban war, and his life had been deeply influenced by the appeal in it.

He had always wanted to make himself strong enough, and true enough, to be able to "carry the message to Garcia." So it was therefore curious that the President should have spoken of this.

As he crossed the square he reviewed his instructions.

The first thing was that he was to leave for Europe on the *Olympic* the following week, accompanied by his faithful servant Fergusson, who had been with him all through the war.

David's war record was outstanding, just as his business record in New York had been outstanding before that. And now, at thirty-three years old, he had this one last task to accomplish before he could retire into private life, and give his time, and his talents, to his country's Government.

"You will have to disappear completely for two months, Major Lamont," the Minister had said. "You can give no account of your movements to anyone—and by the way, avoid meeting old friends or entering into any new acquaintanceships.

"You will receive full instructions at the Embassy in Paris, where you will arrive in twelve days' time, and then you will proceed to carry them out."

His destination lay "somewhere in the Near East," and Fergusson would have everything ready to start. He was accustomed to sudden movements on the part of his master.

David was going to stay in Washington until the night train to New York left. He had an hour now to spare, and would go to see an old friend of his family who lived out on Massachusetts Avenue.

He was very good-looking, although some people thought that he was too stern of countenance for his age, but no one disputed his charm.

David's hair was black and immensely thick, and he wore it brushed back from his broad brow. His skin was clear and his eyes were so dark that the pupils seemed to merge into the irises.

Women adored him. He was quite uninterested in them except as pastimes on the rarest occasions. He had none of the American male tolerance for all their failings. He saw them as they were, without glamour, and utterly despised most of them.

The memory of an adored mother, who had died in the first year of the war, kept his ideal very different from the fluffy bobbed-haired flappers whom he met whenever he dragged himself into society.

David Lamont knew Europe as well as America, and he was no raw novice but a polished man of the world.

He was ruthless and often hard, but he amounted to something, and no one ever talked with him for five minutes without being aware of it, although he had not one touch of egotism and never spoke of himself or of his doings.

"He will go far," some of the Supreme War Council had said, when he was with them in France.

But fate seems to send human beings into back waters sometimes, in spite of all their will, and when David left France in 1920 he had, on his father's death, been swamped in the bog of private business, and it was only now, a year afterwards, that he was able to emerge and take an active part in the game he had set himself to play.

As he ran up the steps of Mrs Longton's house he met an old English friend, Captain Jack

Lumley, who was over on Government business. They had fought together when David was attached to an English Guards Battalion in 1918.

"Hullo, Jack."

"Hello, David, old boy," and they grasped hands and talked for a few moments.

"I'm going back on the *Olympic*—I was just going to wire you in New York."

"I'm crossing on her too," David said, and at that moment the door was opened, and calling out, "So long!" he disappeared inside the house, and Captain Lumley went on down the street with a set face.

An hour ago Jack Lumley had gone to Mrs Longton's on purpose to see Laline Lester, with whom he was deeply in love. She had come in with her Aunt, Mrs Greening, to say farewell before starting for Europe, her first visit abroad.

Laline Lester was all that a really lovely American heiress should be. Highly educated, with wonderful complexion and eyes and hair. Fair as a lily, and with feet and hands and a taste for dress which could not be surpassed.

She had been thoroughly spoilt and indulged all her life, but kept rather away from the ultra-modern set, so that she lent prestige to parties when she attended them.

Her temperament was speculative. She tried things to find if there was any good in them, and when they disappointed her she threw them away.

She had had the usual number of flirtations that every beautiful American heiress of twenty-two has experienced, and she had found them all Dead Sea fruit, and of no meaning.

She had never cared for anyone in her life, except her cat, Mumps, and her mother's old maid, Celestine, with whom she had spoken

French since she was born. Celestine really meant something to her.

The war had prevented her going to Europe during those years, and then had come her mother's death, which had caused no one any grief, since she had been a selfish, hypochondriacal nervous wreck, for as long as her daughter could remember.

Laline was looking for something in life, but she did not know what. All the men she had met she could rule.

She danced with them, listened to their love declarations, realised that they were all the same, and then troubled herself no more about them! She was accustomed to their devotion, which contained no thrill.

Jack Lumley had been different. First, because he was of another nation, so that his methods of trying to gain her favour were not the same. Second, because he had a fine and dear character, and Laline knew it.

But when the pleasure of possessing a new kind of slave had dulled a little, all interest went, and he too joined the throng of those who could not hold her. Only perhaps he was the thing she was fondest of, next to Mumps and Celestine!

That afternoon as they had sat on the sofa in Mrs Longton's smaller drawing-room, Jack had once more asked her to marry him.

He had plenty of money of his own, and was heir to an old cousin's Earldom, and Laline rather wanted to become important in England, as her friend Molly Beaton had become.

She thought that she was very foolish to refuse him, but she just couldn't bring herself to promise anything.

"You know that I don't love you really," she

had said. "If you could ask me again when I am twenty-five, and if I haven't found anyone who can make me feel by then, I'll probably say yes, but it is three years to wait! Oh, Jack, I do want to *feel!*"

His kind blue eyes gazed at her. How he loved her! Every bewitching curl of golden hair, every soft curve of her pink velvet cheeks, every flash of her grey eyes, which seemed to look out resentfully from their brown curly lashes.

Laline's lashes always filled men with a desire to kiss them, they were such babyish things, not the least black, but golden near the skin, turning to brown at the tips. They were so luxuriant, and turned right up against her lids.

Her great green eyes always seemed to be looking out through a shadow that was soft and a little dusky.

Why could not *one* of these would-be husbands make her *feel?*

Molly Beaton had said that Englishmen were very masterful, not a bit good and biddable like American men, and that her own husband was a selfish brute, whom she adored!

So Laline had been much hopeful when Jack Lumley had been presented to her. But he went down under her spell in the first half-hour, and showed as much eagerness to please her as the rest of them had!

When she had said no again, for the third time, as she sat upon Mrs Longton's sofa, Jack Lumley had kissed her very beautiful hands.

"Laline, I love you—you can never know how much. Some people think of love in one way, some in another. For me it means devotion. I would rather you were happy than have my own heart's desire."

"Jack, you dear!"

"I'll wait then, darling, but you'll let me take care of you on the *Olympic* next Wednesday, won't you?"

"Why, certainly . . ."

Then she let him kiss her two hands again, and when he went she rose and looked out the window to watch him as he left the house, and she sighed.

But then her eyes caught sight of David Lamont talking to him, and some slight feeling of interest permeated her. Here was a new type, someone she had never seen before, no native of Washington.

He was dressed in English clothes, very well set up, American assuredly, but of the world.

Who could he be? A friend of Jack's! How warm their greeting was! She could see everything from behind the net curtain. What black hair!

"I hate black hair, and that blue mark where he shaves! Just like an Italian waiter!"

Then she knew that he had entered the house, and in an instant would probably be passing through the room. She was quite alone; her considerate hostess had imagined she was still talking to Captain Lumley and had left her in peace, in this small outer drawing-room.

She certainly felt interested as the butler opened the door and the tall, upright, lithe figure strode in, and passed her with the utmost indifference.

His goal was the farther room, where Daisy Longton could be seen beyond the tea cups and cocktail glasses.

In her whole life, no man in any room had ever passed Laline Lester with indifference!

A little feeling of resentment rose in her. She would stay there, and not return to the others as she had meant to!

Mrs Longton was meanwhile greeting Major Lamont effusively. He was so difficult to secure, and she felt so delighted that he had spared the time to look her up!

She introduced him to a number of pretty girls and their admirers.

"What a frightful bore this custom of introduction is," David thought. "Why in the world can't they do as they do in Europe, and leave people alone!"

How could he ever remember all their tiresome names and their tiresome faces! He had come there to talk to Daisy Longton about old times, and their mutual interests, for they had been children together.

He had not come to be launched into a bunch of debutantes, the very sight of whom irritated him!

They said all the bright things they always said, and smoked and sipped their cocktails, and most of them failed to perceive the amused contempt which lay in Major Lamont's fathomless eyes.

"He is just too darling!" one beauty whispered to her friend, who snapped her head off:

"I think he's a brute, and he makes me feel uncomfortable!"

Laline, alone in the outer room, was becoming more and more disturbed. Was *no one* remembering her absence? The colour deepened in her cheeks. She got out her lapis-and-diamond vanity box and examined herself in the little mirror.

Then she dabbed her white velvety nose and pink velvety cheeks with powder. It would look odd if he passed through again and she was still there alone! So she controlled her resentment at the turn things had taken, and walked through the archway into the inner drawing-room.

Major Lamont looked up as the slender figure came forward to the tea table by which he sat with the hostess. Here was a new flapper was his first thought.

No, she was not a flapper, there was not that jaunty air of knowing childishness, which the rest affected. Also, she was dressed with greater dignity, and her skirts were not quite up to her knees.

All this happened in April 1921, when those who wanted to be dressed as twelve-year-old kiddies had ample opportunity to indulge their fancy, even if they were over forty years old!

She was not painted either, only a little powder, and her lips were innocent of crimson salve. David Lamont was not an out-of-date person.

He had no objection to lip salve or to rouge, or to eye black, when they were an improvement, but in a young girl it seemed a treat to see nature again, as nature in this case was beautiful enough to be left alone!

Yes, this was really a lovely creature, whoever she might be, he decided, and he did not feel so bored when the inevitable introduction took place.

Laline for her part was full of resentment, and did not analyse that she was resenting the very thing which she had longed for—to meet someone who could make her feel!

For she was thrilling with interest in the newcomer, only that her tactics with men were always to appear indifferent, which had been easy hitherto, because it was what she had felt.

But now she was not indifferent, and so she had to act, but the unusualness of it all made her nervous, and she said something that was banal, and Major Lamont answered in the same way, but he watched her.

His black eyes saw through people. He knew she was nervous, and not stupid, and he wondered what had caused this state of mind.

Someone said something about the journey across the Atlantic, and Laline turned to him.

"I am going with my Aunt to Europe on the *Olympic* next Wednesday," she told him. "It is my first visit over there, and I am terribly excited about it!"

So they would be crossing together! But he did not inform her of his plans.

"You are going to Paris, of course."

"Yes, but why 'of course'?"

"All good Americans, especially if they are lovely ladies, go to Paris, as it is the Mecca for clothes!"

Laline pouted. There was something faintly contemptuous or was it only mocking, in his tone?

"I am crazy to see the Art Galleries."

"You are?"

"Why not?"

He smiled, and he knew she was becoming annoyed.

"I'll bet you any amount of money that you will do the Louvre in half-an-hour, spend one afternoon picnicking at Versailles without going near the Palace, and that the rest of the time you'll be at the races or the polo or trying on at the dressmakers' in the Rue de la Paix, and you will dance all night in the Bois or at Montmartre!"

Laline's eyes flashed between their soft lashes.

"If that is what people do in Paris, I shall of

course follow their lead, for it is awful to be a back number! Is that how you spend your time?"

"It depends upon whom I am with."

He looked round at all the pretty silly faces, and he laughed softly to himself.

Laline had never felt so insulted in her life! He had said nothing impertinent, but it was his light and amused tone, and his implication!

Here was the first man who plainly was not dazzled by her, and plainly classed her with all the other girls, just one of a foolish bevy of thistledown!

"Have a cigarette," she suggested, to hide her annoyance, and she opened her case, a companion one to her vanity box, in lapis with her initials in diamonds.

"I hardly ever smoke," he answered, "sometimes a cigar now and then."

"Don't you approve of it?"

He did not reply to this but asked:

"What do you smoke for?"

Laline was nonplussed. She was not quite sure what were her reasons.

"Because it makes you feel good; I can't do anything in the morning until I have had my cigarette," she blurted out.

"Poor slave!"

Rage was rising in Laline.

"I'm not a slave! I only smoke about ten a day."

"Yes, you have just admitted it. You can't do anything until you have had one; therefore, the cigarette is the master, not you!"

"I could stop smoking tomorrow if I liked."

"I should, then: it will be a new experience for you to be the ruler."

This was more than could be borne. A new

experience for her to be the ruler! She, who had ruled everybody all her life!

She told him so, and grew more and more furious at the laughter in his eyes.

"There is obviously one person I am sure you have never succeeded in bringing under your dominion." He was not looking at her as he said this, but absently at a splendid paradise plume in her Aunt's hat, and Laline followed the direction of his eyes, and laughed.

"Auntie! Oh, you have made a mistake there. I can do just what I please with her!"

David turned now, and his black eyes seemed to see right through her golden head.

"'Auntie'? Oh, the lady with the paradise—I wasn't thinking of her!" he exclaimed.

"Who did you mean then?" Laline asked.

"Since you ask, I meant yourself!"

Laline bristled all over.

"I think you are very rude."

"I am sorry, but you asked me, you know." Then he turned away to Mrs Longton again and Laline felt as if she should burst into tears. She had never hated anyone so much before.

Major Lamont was rising to go. She had gathered he was returning immediately to New York. She would never see him again, most probably, and a good thing, and yet . . . ?

"We are going to be at the Ritz-Carlton until we sail. If you want to be rude to me again, you can come, or telephone, and . . ."

He bowed, and there was an amused smile in his eyes, but he did not say if he would come or not.

Mrs Greening had been conversing with him before Laline had entered the room, and she was now effusive in her *adieu*.

"Why, I'm just crazy about that boy, Laline," she said as they went motoring back to Mrs Greening's mansion. "Aren't you?"

"No, I am not!" snapped her niece. "I think he is just as rude as he can be."

* * *

Major Lamont arrived at the dock early on Wednesday and went on board the *Olympic* before the rush began.

He was quietly smoking a cigar on the top deck when, with all the paraphernalia of rich Americans leaving for Europe, Laline and her Aunt and Jack Lumley came across the gangway.

"So old Jack's in tow!" David thought as he watched them. "Laline probably plays with every man!"

He wondered why the thought irritated him!

David kept out of everyone's way all that first afternoon, and he was eating his dinner in a secluded corner in the restaurant when the Greening party came in rather late.

Laline saw him at once out of the corner of her eye. Neither Jack nor her Aunt had noticed him.

David *must* have known that he would be crossing with them, and yet he had never said one word in Washington! What a horrid man!

It was plain to be seen now that he was deliberately avoiding them, and her cheeks burned with annoyance!

From where she sat, the others had their backs to him, and she could look at his profile all the time, unobserved by him. It was a very handsome profile, she was obliged to own, and too there was something so very distinguished about him.

What on earth could he be thinking about so deeply that he never turned round or looked about him?

Of course he would be finished long before they would. Why had her Aunt taken so long to dress?

"Laline dear, you have not heard a word that I have been saying," Mrs Greening remarked plaintively.

"Yes, I have, Auntie, but I'm interested in this new scene."

Jack Lumley had been wondering too at her silence, though he was accustomed to her moods, and knew it was wiser not to remark upon them!

Yes, Major Lamont was getting up now, and they had not reached their ices! He was going through the door into . . . was it perhaps the verandah where people had coffee?

He would have his coffee there, and so should they! She had better talk now, since she need not watch any longer!

"By the way, Jack, I had always meant to ask you, what is the history of the man I saw you speaking to outside Daisy Longton's window? He came in afterwards, and his name is Major Lamont."

"Old David! So you met him! He's a great pal of mine—we were together in the trenches."

"Is he really a soldier or only a war-time one?"

"No, he wasn't a soldier before, and afterwards I think he had something to do with the Intelligence, but he is one of the bravest chaps I've ever come across. He ought to have been on this ship, but I expect he has been delayed. I have not seen him on board at all."

Laline could hardly prevent herself from saying, "Yes, he is here, and over there on the verandah!"

But she smiled blankly and changed the conversation.

Why did her Aunt want all those strawberries for dessert? It was quite a quarter-of-an-hour since Major Lamont had finished his dinner. It was simply ridiculous to take up so much time in eating!

At last, however, they did move, but when they got onto the verandah David was not there! He must have gone on out by the other door!

Laline felt a queer sensation of rage, and soon made an excuse and led her party through all the saloons, but Major Lamont was not seen again that night.

* * *

David Lamont at this stage was not really interested in Laline Lester. In him there was a Pan-like spirit of teasing and it had given him a sort of schoolboy pleasure to be able to get a rise out of her in Washington—and that was all.

She appeared a product of the present-day's lovely, spoilt, over-indulged young womanhood, who could be of no interest to any thinking man, except from one aspect, and he was much too busy to bother with such things at the moment.

He had not even remembered her invitation during the few days he had been in New York, and knowing he would see Jack Lumley on the *Olympic,* he had not concerned himself about him either.

Therefore, as he sat on the verandah drinking his coffee that first evening out, he was asking his inner consciousness why the sight of his old friend, and the two ladies, had given him some sense of vague irritation.

"What animals we are after all!" he said to himself. "I suppose it is because the girl is so darned good to look at, the hunting instinct rises in me, to wrest her from old Jack!"

Then he frowned. He was to avoid new acquaintances, and not even to consort much with old ones.

They would be coming in certainly in a few minutes, and the verandah of the restaurant was not large enough for him to keep aloof from such a friend as Jack Lumley!

So, reluctantly, he finished his coffee and escaped to the smoking-lounge. He became immersed in his book on the history of the country which was to be his destination, which he had brought with him.

Much later, Jack came in alone and found him.

"David! So you are here after all!"

"Why, yes! I was waiting until you weren't a squire of dames, old man. I am fed up with the ubiquitous females of my own country!" He laughed irritably.

A cloud came into Jack's mild blue eyes; he did not like to hear his goddess included in this category.

"Miss Lester and her Aunt are two of the most delightful people one could meet," he announced a trifle stiffly.

"Granted."

"Mrs Greening has taken my cousin's place in Kent near Dover, you know Channings Priory, and they are going there for the summer, after they have done Paris and London."

"They will fill the house with inappropriate guests, and drive the servants all wild, but I suppose they'll double the rent."

Jack laughed now as he sat down and lit a cigarette.

"You are in the devil of a bad temper, David! What's up? And what are you over for this time?"

"Just for a whiff of Paris, and I've got to see my tailor in London; curious how the very best of them lose their cut when they migrate!"

Then they talked of sport for half-an-hour—David had hunted for a season in Leicestershire before the war.

"So you won't make a fourth at our little table of three for meals, David?" Jack laughed as they were leaving the room to turn in.

"No, I *won't!* I am on board to work, and to rest! Good-night!"

* * *

Laline Lester woke rather late the next day with a fixed determination in her mind—the conquest of Major Lamont.

Not, she told herself, that he attracted her in the very least, but just to show him that he could not put over any of that indifference stunt on her!

Men were her natural servants, and she did not mean to stand insubordination from one of them!

She was so glad that she had this lovely trousseau of steamer clothes! A change for every day of the six days! And each tweed or woolly costume and great enveloping fur-trimmed wrap was more becoming than the last!

This morning she would wear the mauve

wool, and a bunch of Parma violets. (Countless boxes of flowers reposed in the chilled chamber, waiting to be brought out fresh for each day of the whole voyage).

What a mercy it was not rough, because after all, since she had never been on the ocean before, she could not be sure what effect it might have upon her!

Jack had assured her that their chairs were in the very best position, out of draughts, on the lee side.

She would not wait for her Aunt, who had the state-room next door, with the bathroom between. She would send for Celestine at once, and get up directly she had eaten her breakfast.

Major Lamont must certainly take exercise, and Jack would in consequence find him during the morning, and then they would meet whether he liked it or not!

Jack's note arrived at that moment:

> *A divine sun!*
> *I will wait for you at the top of the stairs by the lift.*
> > *Jack*

And in less than an hour she stood beside him, an entirely bewitching picture in the mauve suit, her adorable feet in the neatest of grey suede shoes and immaculate silk stockings.

She seemed as fresh as the violets tucked into her belt, and full of joyous anticipation.

Fond love suffused Captain Lumley's eyes. Everything was arranged for her when they reached the chairs, rugs, and cushions, and the deck stewards were just bringing round the chicken broth.

"I think we ought to walk," Jack remarked. "You can sleep all the afternoon."

There was no Major Lamont in sight. A walk, and a thorough investigation of the geography of the ship, would be an excellent thing.

Many eyes followed the pair with interest and admiration, as the usual tramp began. Laline was so radiant a being, with that apple-blossom skin and golden hair. The pink in her cheeks was clear as a wild rose, and deepened in the soft wind.

But they had been round and round the deck four times, and not a sight of any very tall black-haired American gentleman did they see.

Surely he could not be still sleeping. He was not! He was striding on boat deck above them, and when at last Laline suggested that she wanted to be taken up there, and David caught sight of them advancing in his direction, it seemed that a meeting was inevitable.

He quickened his pace, as though upon some special errand, and when they did come face to face he bowed, and would have passed, but Laline stopped and held out her hand.

"Why, what a surprise, Major Lamont! You, going to Europe too!"

"Yes, the call of the cafés in the Bois has lured me there!"

His annoyance at having been caught, when to avoid them he had deliberately abandoned his usual ocean habit of putting in some good miles on A-deck before lunch, to mount to the boat deck where the space was more cramped, made his voice rather acid.

The girl was damnably pretty here in the morning light, and her eyes were full of a challenge, and the blood ran faster in David Lamont's veins than was usual with his compatriots, who were obsessed with business.

"Come and trot with us, you old bear," Jack said. "Miss Lester does not know any ocean liner, and I have never been on a White Star before. But you know the ropes, show us round."

David gave his old friend's arm a nasty tweak, but he had to turn with them and talk lightly, as travellers do.

Laline showed herself intelligent, and did not ask too many feminine and foolish questions.

She was gay as a young lark, and endeavoured to draw Major Lamont into a controversy, but he remained taciturn, and when they had explored the whole of the boat deck, he stopped near the companion ladder.

"You can't get lost now," he growled. "I am going to see how the run is." And without more ado he left them.

"What a difficult man!" Miss Lester pouted. "He's as sure of himself and as disagreeable and gruff as an Englishman!"

"Thanks!" Jack laughed.

"Oh, well, I don't mean you, you're different!"

Down in her heart she was exceedingly annoyed and, for the first time, not quite sure of herself.

David Lamont, as he gained the smoking-room, was annoyed too, for he also did not feel quite on firm ground.

Salt air, May sunshine, blue sea, grey eyes, and pink velvety cheeks, to say nothing of a cupid's-bow cherry mouth that was not painted, were upsetting factors!

He said the word "Garcia" to himself. He was

"carrying a message to Garcia"! Confound the girl!

He did not emerge until luncheon, and then he came into the restaurant so late that the other party were almost leaving.

They nodded, and then David began ordering his food in his casual way of indifference, which Laline so resented. Major Lamont should be annihilated and rendered the merest slave to her whims!

Now she must use her cute business sense, inherited from that successful father of hers, and devise a plan for this man's subjection!

So she passed David's table without even looking at him as they went out, and on deck she allowed herself to be tucked up in her chair by Jack and then pretended to go to sleep, and finally really fell asleep, before Major Lamont came out to pace with Judge Whitmore.

And as he passed and repassed, the most insane desire flooded him to go over and kiss those curly golden brown eyelashes and crush the little fragile body in his strong arms!

So a scowl settled upon his stern face, and even Jack, who joined him in his tramp, did not dare to chaff him.

That night at dinner he felt it prudent to ask the old Judge to share his meal, and as they discussed international politics he succeeded in banishing all thoughts of the other party from his mind.

Laline was burning with fury. It could not *possibly* be that he was really unattracted by her? He must be only acting. Whose will would prove the strongest?

Chapter
Two

Three days passed and the fight went on, and outwardly David Lamont was the complete victor. Nothing which Laline Lester could do, and her arts were great in the way of allurement, could provoke any response from him.

He talked when he was absolutely dragged into talking with her, he seldom looked at her, he never gave her the satisfaction of knowing that he appreciated her marvellous changes of costume, and he gave her always the feeling that she was of no account.

That was the strength of his character; but, underneath, he was growing to be profoundly affected by her. As for the girl, by the last evening before they got into Cherbourg, she had fallen deeply in love with him.

She had asked fate to let her feel, and now it seemed her request had been granted!

Jack, with the sixth sense of men who love, felt this, and his brave heart sank. David, he knew, was not the sort of chap to make any woman happy. He was the best of fellows, but action was his motto, not devotion.

No woman would ever rule him, and no woman would ever come before his duty, or his career.

And as Jack saw, or rather sensed, that Laline was falling in love with his friend, he began to watch and analyse him more and more. He did not feel bitter, for his jealousy took a different form—he felt that he must protect his love from something which could not bring her happiness.

On the fourth night out, a sharp wind had arisen and the next day it was very rough.

Laline woke convinced that she was a perfect sailor by now! She rose before her usual time, feeling that she could not be hidden in her cabin this last day, when there was no knowing if she would ever see Major Lamont again once they landed.

She had not been able to extract from him if he was really coming to Paris or going on to Southampton.

Celestine was entirely *hors de combat,* and Laline was obliged to dress alone. She rammed her gold curls into a soft cap and put on a big cloak.

She was conquering as well as she could a very unusual and unpleasant feeling! The air was all she craved! Where was Jack? Why had he not been to see how she was?

She grew peevish, and then she found that it was half-an-hour earlier than Jack was accustomed to expect her. He was quite blameless, but she felt as cross with him as if it had been his fault!

She staggered as she got into the corridor. Their state-rooms were on B-deck, but she managed to get up the stairs safely. If she could only reach her chair! All would be well.

Dimly she perceived Major Lamont coming

out of his cabin, which was just at the corner of the square hall on A-deck.

What was going to happen? What awful things? She felt as though she were dying. He must not see her . . . Oh! heavens, not that . . .

She made one wild rush for the open lee-side door . . . and then subsided into the arms of a friendly steward, who caught her as she fell!

David had an idea what was likely to have happened, and with great discretion went out on the deck by the opposite side, where the wind was strong and the sky blue and pitiless. He felt he could not face disillusionment!

But presently his walk took him to the lee-side, for he felt she would have gone below by this time, but no—there was a huddled little figure all alone, without a scrap of colour in the soft cheeks, and with the air of an unhappy child.

Politeness obliged him to stop and say something cheery.

"Oh! Do come and take care of me!" Laline almost whimpered. "Jack has never appeared, and I hate it."

David took the empty chair at her side. He knew Jack was not a bad sailor, and would be with them very shortly, and there was no use in arguing with himself about it, he wanted to sit beside her!

"Keep your eye on the horizon," he told her; "that makes you feel all right at once."

"I had no idea the sea could be such a yellow dog!"

A little colour came back into Laline's cheeks with the joy of having David near her! She was praying now that Jack was ill, bad enough to keep him in his cabin all the morning!

"The sea is as capricious as a woman," David said.

"I don't think women are the least capricious, they only know what they want, and generally get it. . . ."

"And then when their vanity is appeased, they throw the thing away."

"That is not caprice, that is method, and having a sense of values."

"A thing becomes valueless, then, when you have secured it?"

"Yes, often. I hardly ever want what I have got, and I long for the unattainable."

"What an uncomfortable instinct in the home!" He laughed rather cynically.

"I suppose it would be, but I haven't a home yet . . . Auntie and I have given instructions to sell the house in Washington, and if I find I like Paris we'll settle there."

"Jack tells me you have taken his cousin's place, Channings Priory, for the summer. I wonder what the English life will say to you?"

"I shall most probably be crazy about it."

"Until something new turns up."

"Yes."

"What is that book you are reading there?"

"It is called *This Side of Paradise*. It is awfully like us all, isn't it; have you read it?"

He had. He looked at her just a trifle savagely.

"Do you let all your partners kiss you like that?" he asked boldly.

Laline forgot that she had felt ill, and triumph came to her.

"He's jealous," she thought. "In spite of himself!"

"No . . . only the nicest." Her grey eyes grew enticing.

A rush of passion came to him. He knew that he wanted to kiss her there and then, and if they had been alone, he would certainly have done so.

But people were walking up and down, although the chairs on either side were untenanted, so that no one could hear their conversation.

He bent over her, and for the first time she saw a look in his eye!

Her cheeks were wild roses once more, and it is impossible to know what he would have said, because at that moment Fergusson came out onto the deck, a Marconigram in his hand.

His manner was one of icy respect, and it pulled up his master with a jerk as he took the envelope. He seemed to see the word "Garcia" floating before his eyes.

Fergusson knew the gravity of his mission, and his taciturn character would certainly, and rightly, disapprove of any amorous interludes! David felt angry with himself, and very angry with the bewitching little temptress!

He got up abruptly after reading the message.

"I must go and attend to this, but I'll beat up Jack and send him to you. *Au revoir!*"

Laline could have cried. She hated Fergusson, she hated Marconigrams, she hated even Jack, who appeared at that moment, full of contrition.

"Darling baby, why did not you tell me you were coming up so early on this beastly morning?"

Tears of disappointment, augmented by unpleasant bodily sensations, were in Laline's eyes.

David had gone, and what if fate were going to overcome her again . . . ? Oh! The sea . . . !

Nothing could exceed Jack's tenderness and

care; *he* did not run the other way! A mother could not have been more concerned and soothing.

He took her down to her state-room, and helped the stewardess to put her to bed, and then sat there and held her hand until she went to sleep. And by luncheon-time the wind had dropped, and there was every prospect of a beautiful last evening ahead.

David and Jack ate together in the restaurant, neither of the ladies being present. And in his heart each man was thinking of the same thing—how he should spend the time with a certain golden-haired, spoilt girl!

Jack had made the usual plan. She would come up to tea, and then they would take a walk, and then sit in their chairs and watch the sunset.

David was being deliberate with himself; he meant to allow himself one whole hour's pleasure. It should be no more than an hour, and then he would cut out the whole thing.

He had no intention of being weak, and besides, an hour could not hurt any man! He did not make a plan, because he knew he could just take her when he wanted her. Action was his motto!

"You'll make a perfect husband, Jack. Why haven't you married?" David asked.

"I hope to, someday. But now I'm devoted to someone!"

"You are a devoted creature altogether; they don't deserve it. I'm not."

"No, old son, you represent the cave man, and they'll love you far better than they will ever love me!"

"I suppose I am a brute." David laughed. "I am some kind of dynamic force and I can't help it."

Laline was determined to make herself look exquisite for tea in her last steamer-outfit. It was a misty grey-blue this time. She felt quite well again. Celestine had recovered too, and could do her hair.

Her Aunt meant to rest. Therefore, she could dress in peace, after a lovely hot bath, and send for Jack to take her to her chair. And if she could not get Major Lamont to make love to her, well, she was not worth a ten-cent piece!

*   *   *

It was unlikely that, Laline determining to subjugate Major Lamont, and David having allowed himself the prospect of one hour to amuse himself in, fate should not smile upon them.

The three had tea together in the saloon, and then Laline sent Jack down to implore Mrs Greening to join them at their chairs, to watch the sunset.

The moment that the kind fellow's back was turned, she raised soft eyes to Major Lamont, and suggested that they should go up on the boat deck for a few minutes first, and see how the great orange sun looked from there.

She was not at all sure that he would consent; and indeed, had he not arranged his plan, he would have been quite capable of refusing point blank.

Her hesitation gave a new charm to her sparkling face.

"It's a great idea," David answered. "Let's!"

So they stole away, and up the stairway, and on to the farthest point of the boat deck, and there leaned over the rail and gazed to the west.

The soft wind, which had sunk to a mere zephyr by now, played with the golden tendrils of

Laline's hair, and never had she appeared more delectable.

David allowed himself to bend quite close to her.

"Oh, isn't it gorgeous!"

He did not answer, he just looked at her, and his strongly magnetic eyes seemed to enter her very being, and cause some strange fluttering near her heart.

Then he took out his watch and glanced at it. It was ten minutes to six.

"She intends to excite me," he thought.

"Why do you look at your watch?" Laline asked.

"To see how much time I have to look at you."

"Do you want to look at me?"

"Of course. Aren't you extremely good to look at?"

"Yes, but I did not make myself," she pouted, "so that does not amount to anything in the way of a compliment!"

"You only like to be flattered about that over which you have will, then?"

"Why certainly!"

He remained silent.

This exasperated her, for she made the deduction that he did not find so much to praise on this point! There was a question and a challenge in her eyes.

"Well, why don't you say something?"

"I'm a bear and I can only tell the truth!" He laughed.

"And you think that I would not like it?" She was getting angry.

"Probably not."

"Try!"

"No, I won't."

"I order you to!"

"Order as much as you like."

"You won't obey?"

"No."

"Brute!"

"Honey!"

"I'm not 'honey' to you . . . you are always rude and hateful to me!"

"Why did you suggest coming up on this deck, then?"

"On the same principle that one takes bitters before dinner . . . an aperitif."

She laughed. There was no use in growing mad with him—she knew that she would get the worst of it.

"Well, it is better to be that than a chocolate ice-cream."

"Do you mean Jack?"

"No, Jack is the best fellow in the world, far too good for modern flappers to worry between their teeth!"

"Am I to understand that you are insinuating that I am a modern flapper, Major Lamont?"

"Not exactly, you have escaped the worst form of their expression, but the flapper epidemic has gone so deep in our country, it seems that hardly a woman under fifty escapes entirely from its influence."

"What do you just mean by the 'flapper epidemic'?"

She was trying to be reasonable, and not to show her growing irritation.

"Well, putting over every impossible bad taste and unattractive 'sassiness' under the excuse of infantile years."

"And you think it has caught me?" Her voice almost trembled.

"Partly."

"How dare you say such things!"

"You asked me a deliberate question."

"Then you have just got to explain yourself."

"You wouldn't understand."

"You are absolutely insulting, Major Lamont! The implication of everything you have said is that I am an empty-headed, posing girl, with not enough horse sense to comprehend plain English!"

"When the head is as pretty as yours, it does not matter what is inside it!" He laughed good-humouredly.

"It matters a whole lot! You have made a great mistake; I am neither a flapper nor empty-headed! But why I tolerate your insolence, I don't know."

"I do."

"You do!"

"Yes. It is because you know that I would not attempt to hold you if you bolted away!"

"Well, why did you come up on this deck, then? It could not have been only to insult me, you had some other reason."

"Yes, I had. I wanted to enjoy the pleasure of looking at you in the very few moments that I mean to spare."

"You only want to look at, and not to talk to, girls then?"

"Generally they have not much that it is interesting to discuss in their heads, which are only filled with themselves, and their own vanity."

"You are frightfully unjust. We are, as a rule,

ten times better educated and more intelligent than
you men."

"Then it is all the more a shame that you
make so little use of it. If you are rich enough not
to have to work, the whole force goes to drawing
incense for your vanity and learning new tricks
to kill time."

Then he laughed softly. He had not meant to
have any serious conversation with her. He did not
think her brain was worth it, she was merely a
pleasure, but such a very great pleasure that he
would have to be careful about it all.

The hunting instinct, he knew, was terribly
strong in him!

Laline, however, having got her resentment
well in hand, only longed to draw him into a dis-
cussion, so she answered meekly, instead of firing
up:

"What would you have us do, then?"

"For the moment, I would have you let me
hold your arm and walk briskly up and down this
deck!"

"But we were talking in the abstract, and you
bring it down to the particular. . . ."

She was, however, not displeased!

"Much the best thing to do, for the minutes
are passing and I have only allowed myself an hour
for enjoyment!"

"I am an enjoyment, then?"

"Certainly."

"And a temptation, to stray from work?"

"Tremendous!"

"My brain counts nothing at all, you just
want to hold my arm!"

"I neither know nor care if you have a brain.
We have only"—he looked at his watch—"thirty-

five more minutes. Let's get the tangible joy out of a jolly walk and propinquity!"

Laline was in love with David Lamont. She knew it, although she had never been in love before in her life.

She just felt that it did not really matter then if he had been very insulting. The temptation for him to be quite close to her, holding her arm, was greater than her pride.

She knew men very well too, and that the shortest way to their brains and hearts lies most surely through the door of their senses!

So she smiled a divine smile, and made a caressing movement nearer to him, and he took her arm, and they began their walk.

If he felt just the agreeable physical excitement of the way of a man with a maid, Laline experienced much more exalted emotions!

Everything in her was thrilling at his touch. His hold was firm. She suddenly felt her rebellion was silly. Of what matter anything, if such a man loved her!

She would not be able to put up any fight. He might just be complete master, and make her do as he pleased!

David Lamont felt his pulses bounding. "The darling little girl! The little honey, the little sweetheart!" he said to himself. He had not felt so much for over two years!

They talked of foolish things, as light as the evening wind, but at each turn his arm seemed to hold her tighter and more joy and gladness permeated them both.

And David Lamont in his cynical way was analysing to himself:

"It is the spring-time, and all the re-creative

forces are in the air, and after all, if girls could only stay young and lovely and provide this stimulus to man, what on earth is the use of their having any mind?"

This was what women were for, only the darnedest part was that if you took one for this, you might be saddled with a bore when the essential faded!

Laline glanced at her wrist watch. There was only five minutes left, but she was determined to make him stay with her over the time, if it were only for a few seconds! She *would* win on some point! The surrender was too ignominious otherwise.

He also looked at his watch.

"I have four and three-quarter minutes more," he said. "Come." And he drew her rapidly to the end of the deck, where they would be quite alone, by the life-boats.

When they reached the spot where no one could possibly see them, David let go of her arm and seized both her hands.

"I want to kiss you."

The coquette in her fenced.

"Of course! Well, perhaps you shall, if you stay and chuck your old work!"

"No, I am going in four minutes. Let me kiss you now."

"No! The price is for you to wait!"

"I will pay no price. Do you mean to struggle? The seconds are going by!"

The magnetism of his eyes, blazing now with passion, held her. Here was emotion for her, here was feeling! But she must try to rule once more.

So she tossed her golden head and pouted.

"If I am not worth waiting for ... I am not worth kissing!"

"You are probably not, but I am a man, and for the moment you seem worth it to me. I suppose there are only about three minutes now, so why waste them?"

Laline felt everything in her melting as his black eyes held her, and his firm mouth, smiling a little, showed just a white gleam of his perfect teeth.

"Oh!" she gasped, overcome, and he folded her in his arms.

She had never dreamed of such a kiss! She had had others, but they had not meant a thing to her. But this kiss . . . Oh . . .

It seemed to draw her whole being to him. Time and place vanished in one divine thrill.

That anything so passionate, so long, so utterly tender too, could come from that stern, fierce brute David Lamont was too glorious! She knew only that she loved him wildly, adoringly . . . completely.

He picked her up in his arms when at last his lips left hers, and deposited her in a vacant chair.

"Thank you, honey," he whispered, and then turned and left her, striding on, and down the companion stair to A-deck.

When the intoxication quieted a little in Laline, she glanced at her watch; it was within a minute of ten minutes to seven o'clock. He had done as he said. The hour was not yet up!

She felt exhausted, deliciously, divinely exhausted! Her cheeks kept paling and glowing alternately, while her lovely little figure just stayed limp in the chair.

He had kissed her and gone off to work. What was this imperative work? Of course, men must work, but Jack would never have done that!

Just a few minutes more or less could not

have mattered to the horrid old task, whatever it was, and the "more" would have been so perfectly glorious for them!

But there was tonight, and there would be a half-moon . . . and . . . and . . . Oh! she must go down and make herself just as beautiful as she and Celestine, between them, knew how to make her!

She would wear the soft pervenche georgette which was not so very short, and which seemed to turn her grey eyes into dewy hyacinths, so she had been told!

Then with a recrudescence of emotion, she walked on and down the stairs. But as she came nearer the lee-side door, near where their chairs were, what incredible sight met her eyes in the middle distance?

David Lamont, pacing the deck between Judge Whitmore and his tiresome wife, who had only emerged from her cabin that afternoon!

Pacing the deck from the other end, showing that he had been round once already, and must have joined them deliberately on his leaving her! He was not working, then! He could never have intended to work!

The shock was perfectly horrible to her. She went cold all over, and walked forward to the chairs, her head in the air, and her grey eyes like icicles. Before she reached them, the three people came face to face with her.

"Perfect evening for a stroll, Miss Lester," David Lamont called cheerily. "Where's Jack? You should not be so lazy, but tramp as we do!"

Then he went on.

Laline got to her chair and fell into it, her knees almost giving way under her.

*   *   *

Celestine wondered what was the matter with her much-loved mistress and baby.

She knew almost her every thought, and with her mixture of natural French intelligence, and acquired American shrewdness, she divined that something had occurred concerning "ze Major Lamont," whom she was well aware occupied most of her lamb's thoughts.

She had taken pains to acquaint herself with Fergusson, no easy matter, and she had endeavoured to find out from him something of his master's character.

Laline had been her darling, her golden-haired love, from the moment Celestine had taken service with her tiresome, nervous, drug-taking mother, when Laline was but five years old, and to see Laline happy and well established was her one desire.

But as she did her sweet little lady's hair for dinner, some vague feeling of trouble oppressed her.

"Nannie," Laline said, "I am in the hell of a temper, and I want to murder Major Lamont!"

Celestine nodded comprehensively.

"Il est difficile."

"Difficult! *Mon Dieu!* He is impossible . . . of an insolence which no woman could put up with. I shall never speak to him again. . . ."

"That is well."

"Why is that well?"

"Because he is not of a docility like the usual members of *Mademoiselle*'s entourage. He can be made to wear no bridle, and so for happiness it would be wiser for *Mademoiselle* to let him go by."

Laline clenched her hands.

"But the worst of it is, Nannie, the ones who

won't be bridled are the only ones worth bothering about."

"What does *Mademoiselle* mean to do, then?"

Laline lay back with her golden head supported on her beloved Nannie's ample bosom, and said slowly, tears coming into her eyes:

"I love him. That's all!"

"Tiens! Tiens!" protested Celestine. "All love passes. Let it pass soon."

"But I want him."

"Quel malheur!"

"You think I should be unhappy with him?"

"A slave, but merely a slave! *Mademoiselle* has perhaps not observed the mouth of the Major."

"Yes, I have."

"Not for kisses."

"Not . . . for kisses," Laline said, and gasped.

Suddenly a wave of strong emotion swept her. Not for kisses! when not three-quarters of an hour ago he had held her lips in the most divine kiss that could be dreamed of in Paradise!

"That is the perfectly terrible part of it, Celli . . . he is just for the only kisses worth having on earth!"

Laline covered her face with her hands. Then she jumped up, finished her dressing rapidly, and went into her Aunt's cabin.

"I've sent up to ask the Whitmores to join us on our last night," her Aunt announced. "And they have accepted, although they had thought of inviting Major Lamont themselves, so we must ask him too."

"Not a bit of it!" exclaimed Laline. "Let the bear alone. He'd probably refuse, anyway!"

"I thought you liked him, Laline?"

"He bores me now. I walked on the top deck with him after tea. . . ."

"That is why Jack couldn't find you, then! He was so upset, poor boy."

"Oh, it does men good to hurt them!" Laline responded savagely, and went back to her own state-room.

Meanwhile, David Lamont, in his cabin, was smoking one of his rare cigars.

The hour, especially the end of it, had been perfectly delicious. What a little sweetheart the girl was! What skin, what eyes, and what lips!

He did not feel the least contrition for his action. He knew Laline was no timid, trusting country flower, whom he must carefully not lead astray. He believed that she was as equally well equipped as he was himself as an opponent in the game.

But for now, until he had returned to Paris after the two months' duty was over, and he could perhaps look Mrs Greening and her niece up in England, he must have no further intercourse with them.

He must put his whole mind before his work ahead. He had mastered a very difficult code he had been given at Washington; but there remained, of the nation with which he would have to deal, one or two aspects which it would be advisable to study more deeply.

He read for half-an-hour, stretched upon his sofa, but he was unable to prevent his pulses from bounding every now and then, when the remembrance of Laline's soft lips would obtrude itself between the pages.

"I'll have to take a hold on myself," he said.

The Greening, Lumley, and Whitmore party

were seated at their table, and at a second course, when he sauntered into the restaurant.

Laline's place faced him, if he chose to turn his head; if not, she could always see his profile, and not a line or expression of it was unknown to her, after a watch of five days!

Tonight she had that uncomfortable, hot sense of pins and needles at the tips of her fingers when she caught sight of him coming in, and every time she permitted herself to look at him.

There was such easy grace in all his attitudes. His skin was so clean and refined, and she had even grown to like the bluish mark where he shaved his black beard.

But what impudent indifference he was showing tonight! He had a book with him! She grew more and more nervous, and more and more attracted.

David finished his meal before the larger party, and retired at once with his book to a comfortable chair in the saloon.

There they could see him ensconced and absorbed in the pages, when, quite late, they came down there from the restaurant verandah where they had had coffee.

Would he not speak to them *at all* before going to bed?

Laline felt so unhappy by now, she had lost all resentment, and her heart was as heavy as lead. They would get in to Cherbourg quite early in the morning and would probably catch the first train after all; everyone was speculating about it as usual on the last night.

Was he going to get off, or was he going on to Southampton?

It was a perfectly awful thought that a man who had held her in his arms, and given and taken from her the fondest, longest kiss, should be sitting there perfectly indifferent, and that she should not know if they would ever meet again, and she was not even certain if he would say good-night!

She became so nervous at last that she had to hold her little hands together. They were not white as usual, but purplish and icy cold.

Jack *sensed* that she wanted to speak to David.

"I wonder what that old bear is reading so deeply," he said; "I think I'll go and stir him up!"

Laline watched, and saw when Jack reached his friend that he had to be literally shaken from his book. He was not acting, then. He really was interested in it.

The pain seemed to grow round her heart, but there was rage too.

If she had known, David had had a hard fight with himself more than once to keep his attention; visions of the upper deck, and the half-moon, and the possibilities, would come to him —but this is where discipline came in.

He had no intention of succumbing to desire, and he *had* the intention to show no further interest in Miss Lester.

"Come and have a farewell drink, David old boy. The ladies want to say good-bye to you. You are going on to Southampton to see your tailor in London, I think you said?"

David made no reply to this, but in a kind of reluctant way, almost as though he were being dragged, he got up and followed Jack back to the group in one of the little alcoves.

He was perfectly polite and ordinary to everyone; and Laline could hardly keep back tears. She had become so temperamental that if it had been anyone else but David there, she would just have had a break-down, and rushed off to her state-room.

But she would not have dared to show any foolish emotion before him, for that indeed would have been the end of things!

They drank champagne, and she deliberately lit a cigarette, which she had hardly ever done in the last days, when David was near. He must see that she, too, was indifferent! But he did not appear to see anything; he was just aloof.

"If I stay another minute I shall snatch her up and carry her out onto the deck and kiss her to death," he was thinking, so he rose, and wishing them all a casual good-night, he went on to his cabin.

Laline had a sensation that she was going to faint, only Jack came to her rescue, and said some cheery thing, and then suggested that she must be packed off to bed, to be up in time in the morning.

And, because her Aunt did not appear to be wanting to stir, he led her off by herself.

But when he said good-night to her at the state-room door, his kind eyes were full of fondest concern.

"Oh! Jack! You are the greatest dear in this world!" she said, and then she went in and shut the door.

Chapter
Three

Laline gazed idly out the window of the train the next day, after they had left the ship. She could see a road and—what was that? A motor car! A very smart, open Rolls-Royce, and Major Lamont in it! Surely it was he? She could not have been mistaken.

How had he got there? How had he possibly landed without their knowing it, and not bothered with the customs house, and just sailed off in a car?

She was full of mixed feelings, but chief among them was the fact that France suddenly became of more interest to her, and especially the thought of Paris. Perhaps he would be in Paris? Perhaps she would see him again after all.

She did not breathe a word of her discovery to Jack or to her Aunt, who believed that Major Lamont had gone quietly on to Southampton.

But presently she asked Jack, casually, how long it would take to get to Paris by motor, and why they had not thought of going that way.

The whole journey for Laline now became one longing to reach their destination. As the long day drew to a close, and Paris was reached, she was tired and quiet. They were, of course, going to the Ritz. Jack had arranged everything.

By the next morning, refreshed and blooming, and lovely, Laline came down with her Aunt to luncheon in the garden.

They were at one of the tables just beyond the restaurant windows, in the Ritz garden, and all the new atmosphere, and the aspect of the people round, was filling Laline with interest, and food for thought.

"By Jove! There is David!" cried Jack in surprise. "How the deuce did he get here? I thought he was in England!"

The most brilliant rose pink flooded Laline's cheeks. Where . . . where was he? She could not see him!

She tried to control her excitement, and follow the direction of Jack's eyes. Yes, at last she saw him at the other end, standing by an entrance door, looking down the garden towards them.

How smart he was! What a gentleman! How distinguished! How adorable!

He caught sight of the party and bowed calmly, but did not attempt to join them.

Laline's excitement increased. It was this element of uncertainty which caused the powerful effect upon her. Never had she had the satisfaction of feeling secure in one single particular in regard to Major Lamont.

If he had been merely an insolent and indifferent society person, he could not have thus concerned her. It was that strange thing, the magnetic force of a dominant personality, which, being the real thing, and not a pose, made itself felt by everyone approaching it.

She *knew* instinctively that David was in reality everything which she could respect, however his outer indifference annoyed her.

David thought constantly of Laline, but he *must* "carry the message to Garcia." He must *not* allow any new interest to hold him until that mission was completed.

He knew as he sped through France's green country, the air laden with the scents of springtime, that he was more attracted by Laline Lester than he had been by any woman before in his life.

If he only had time, he could find extreme pleasure in endeavouring to discover if there was real gold of character underneath, but he *must* "carry the message to Garcia." He would try not to see them again before he was through with that!

His appointment with the Ambassador was for eleven o'clock the next day.

He went up to his usual rooms at the Ritz, but not at the hour that the Greening party arrived, so there had been no meeting.

And the evening he had spent in carefully arranging and classifying his papers.

He arrived at the Embassy exactly on time on Wednesday. The Ambassador saw him immediately and they had an hour's talk, of deeply satisfactory nature to both men, and at the end of it His Excellency said:

"So you have six whole days' leave from tomorrow, Major Lamont. Do exactly what you please, and have a good time and forget all about your work, only report here to me next Tuesday at twelve o'clock, ready to start at a moment's notice. From Rome onwards, you become an unknown unit!"

David expressed his thanks.

"I wanted to go and have a look at the battlefields."

"In that case, let me lend you a very fast two-seater, which is lying idle in my garage. I have always meant to make some record spins when I had time."

David found this entirely to his taste.

"I want you to dine with us tonight, Lamont; we have a State function for a certain Royalty and his wife who still may be of some use to you in the Near East. Eight-thirty sharp, and afterwards dance in the opening quadrille with my niece, Mrs Hamilton.

"We are going to have the first after-war ceremonial show. Most of us have forgotten quadrilles! It is Her Royal Highness' wish that one is danced, and you I expect know the ropes!"

As David turned away from the door of the Ritz garden, he half-wondered to himself if Laline would be at the Embassy? And if so, if . . . ?

He had six days in which he had been given permission to *forget* duty.

Six days held a good many possibilities. If she was at the Embassy he would take that as an omen that he might amuse himself. If she was not, then he would not bother with any women during the time.

*   *   *

Before Laline and her Aunt had finished luncheon, a note was brought to them from the Embassy. Mrs Randolph, the Ambassadress, was an old friend of Mrs Greening, and was aware of what would be the date of their arrival.

The note was to greet Aunt and niece, and invite them to the Ball that same night for the foreign Royalty; they were to telephone to her directly on receipt of the letter.

Mrs Greening was enchanted to obey the request, and in a conversation with her old friend she secured Jack an invitation.

"So very much nicer to have a man of our own with us, Laline," she said.

And Laline agreed. But she was not thinking of Jack or of anyone, only wondering if David would be there.

The American Embassy! It was quite possible, although perhaps, as the party was for Royalty, they might not ask just a simple Major who was over here on a holiday.

Still, the hope would give an extra reason for making her appearance simply stunning, and if he was there, he would not think she could not do credit to America!

* * *

The American Embassy of that year was in a very fine house in Paris, and the Ambassador and Mrs Randolph knew exactly how to entertain the great ones of the earth.

Orders would be worn, and everything would be done with great state, for the first time since peace had been declared.

Major Lamont's partner for dinner was the Ambassador's niece, a young widow, Mrs Hamilton, who was in Paris for a week or so before going on to Rome.

She was a very pretty, graceful creature, with big brown eyes, and during the banquet David passed an agreeable time with her, even though underneath there was some suppressed excitement in the speculation as to whether or not Laline Lester would arrive afterwards.

Laline had dressed with extreme care, and she was never snappy to Celestine when she was excited, which was one of the dear points about her, and the fond old maid beamed with joy upon her beauty.

Jack and Laline's Aunt both felt that she was the loveliest bit of young womanhood they had ever laid eyes upon, as she came into the sitting-room, ready to start.

She had refused to dine with them down in the restaurant; she wanted the whole time until they were to leave, to rest in, and to dress in, she had said.

So Jack and Mrs Greening had eaten alone, and now she had burst upon them, a vision of spring beauty.

Passionate love was in Jack's mild blue eyes as he put her cloak round her.

"Laline, I love you. I love you!" he whispered. "Are you never going to promise me anything at all?"

"Only what I've always said, Jack. Perhaps someday . . . !"

And then Mrs Greening interrupted them, coming from her room.

"If there are Royalties there we ought to be on time, Laline. We are asked for eleven o'clock, so let's start!"

It happened, however, that they were among the very first to arrive. And so they were just coming up the great staircase as the procession came out of the dining-room and into the great open space of the hall.

The Royal Prince and the Ambassadress, and the Ambassador and the Princess, and then the rest, according to their rank.

Mrs Greening stopped on the top step, and Laline stood beside her, and watched until they all passed, and suddenly the girl's heart gave a great bound, for there was Major Lamont among the great ones of the earth!

He had been asked to dinner, and they only to the hall with the crowd. He was also with a very pretty woman, very pretty, and perfectly dressed, and he would see that they had been so countrified as to arrive so terribly early.

Excitement, humiliation, jealousy, and the usual anguish of uncertainty shook Laline. Always, always, was she at a disadvantage with him.

As the procession passed, and broke up just beyond them, towards the door of the great salon, David caught sight of her lovely little face, with the eyes shining with emotion, and the pink velvety cheeks glowing.

He was conscious of a flood of joy, but he never allowed his feelings to show. So he passed with a polite bow, and Laline's teeth almost chattered with nervous excitement.

The poor child was passionately in love for the first time in her twenty-two years of life. She had never been taught to control any emotion, or to deny herself any and every indulgence.

She saw that the Royal Prince had indicated that David should come and speak to him, and she watched with what perfect ease and self-confidence he obeyed the command.

The Ambassador joined the group, and they seemed to be treating the "simple Major" with every interested respect.

"How well he must know the world!" thought Laline.

Then the Ambassador drew forward the lady

with the brown eyes, and they all seemed to be having a gay conversation, at ease with one another.

The Prince moved on then, and Major Lamont remained with the fascinating lady.

Laline burned with jealousy. This woman had one advantage over her: she evidently knew Europe. But she, Laline, would learn that soon, and *no woman* should eventually put one up on her on that score!

The moment had arrived to go forward, so soon their greetings were made, and the Ambassadress was most cordial. Anything as lovely as Laline must grace her quadrille.

The lady who was to have danced with the second secretary had been ill, and had not come.

Here was the very thing! Immediately she made the arrangement, and introduced the secretary to her.

"I have never danced a quadrille," Laline laughed, "but I suppose unimportant people like us will be at the side, so I'll watch and follow."

She was so glad that David should see that she was not just one of the general crowd. Would he come and speak to her? If only she had the pluck to be "up stage" with him should he do so. But she knew she would never succeed in that.

When the people began to take their places, and the musicians were playing a prelude, David and Mrs Hamilton took up their vis-à-vis to the second secretary and Laline.

This added to Laline's excitement, and to David's pleasure.

How lovely she looked! And how clever of her to have picked up the Paris look so soon!

Yes, fate had answered, and he should follow

the indication, and tomorrow, when his six days should begin, he would arrange to spend some of them with her if possible.

He would keep himself well in hand, but no doubt the affair would develop into a promising flirtation, and perhaps, when he came back . . .

Tonight he would go and talk to her directly the dance should be over, and take her out, and sit in one of the smaller rooms.

Poor dear old Jack! But then she was not bound to Jack, and a woman was fair game, and if Jack could not secure her, it was up to him.

And then the quadrille began.

"He's doing it properly," Laline thought. "I suppose he knows Courts. I do hope I'll be all right."

Would David come and talk to her? As he was close to her in the last turn, he whispered very low:

"Make your partner take you out into the hall."

If anyone else in the world had said such a thing in the tone of a command to Laline, she would have resented it strongly, and would have gone in the opposite direction.

But now her heart beat quickly, and joy rushed over her. She would see him, she would speak to him! Nothing else mattered at all.

Fortunately, she was no novice in manipulating situations, and the obedient second secretary found himself leading his lovely partner into the hall, when he had intended to take her into the music-room beyond the ball-room.

She would have to keep him with her until David appeared.

David had not found it so easy to get rid of

Mrs Hamilton, his companion, who had no intention of letting him go. Only his natural ruthless-
ness and perfect sangfroid aided him.

He deliberately led her past the Royal Prince,
so close that he would be obliged to address her
to him, knowing her to be the Ambassador's niece,
and in that second David bowed, as if dismissed,
and bolted into the crowd.

Laline's foot was tapping the carpet, when he
did come up, and her irritation had begun to rise
again.

"Ah, here you are, Miss Lester!" David exclaimed. "Your Aunt has sent me to fetch you to
be introduced to one of her old friends," he said,
and the polite young second secretary moved
aside.

David ceremoniously gave Laline his arm,
and instead of leading her back into the salon,
where both knew her Aunt was, he drew her across
the hall and into a little room, which contained
only a big sofa, and cases of miniatures, and
bibelots.

It led to the private apartments, and there
they would probably be alone. Laline was enchanted!

He moved one of the cushions for her, and
indicated that she was to sit down. She did, and
leant back against the soft yellow satin, and
opened her giant fan.

David sat down beside her.

"Now tell me all about it," he commanded,
and he took her little left hand and deliberately
began to pull the glove off it.

Laline made as though she would resist him,
but his firm grasp tightened on her wrist.

"I don't want the glove; I want to kiss the
palm."

"Major Lamont, you are really too impertinent!" she said with a gasp, but her voice was not as indignant as it ought to have been.

His touch was magnetising her, destroying her power to resist him. He understood everything that she was feeling, and he delighted in it.

"Now begin."

"Begin what?" She was still pulling back her hand.

"Begin to tell me all about everything you have done, and said, and thought of, since I left those adorable lips on the *Olympic*'s top deck. But it is perfectly useless for you to struggle about your hand. I mean to hold, and kiss it, as I want."

"Flabbergasted" is the only word which can describe Laline's state of mind. Here, with supreme disregard of the indifference, the insulting indifference, which he had shown in between times, he was going right back to the evening of the kiss as though they had not since met.

"I should not have thought anything about me interested you," she said, pouting, but her resistance grew less, and now, beyond making her fingers stiff and uncompromising, she did not struggle to remove her hand from his grasp.

"How silly of you!" He began to kiss each little pink-nailed finger. "You ought to have known that I was thinking of you all the time."

He pressed his lips to her palm. A sensation of intoxication was stealing over Laline, the curious thrill of love when it is holding the senses. She *could not* take her hand away. Her red mouth smiled softly, and her eyes were dewy.

David had the profound temptation to clasp her in his arms, and kiss her lips once more, but his fastidiousness would not let him. Not here, at an Embassy, with the chance of someone coming in.

He had awakened something within her, which is what he had intended to do, so now he put her hand back in her lap.

"You are utterly sweet, honey," he said.

"And you are a perfect brute."

"Yes, I know, but don't let's quarrel in our short time of grace. Forgive everything, and let us start fair. Tell me what you are going to do in Paris, especially tomorrow."

She did try to be dignified, but it was impossible to feel angry any more. She was just throbbing with love!

"We have not settled anything."

"Then I suggest a plan. I have had a two-seater lent me, for six days, and I am going to see the battlefields. Why don't you come with me, and make old Jack and your Aunt, and anyone else they want, join us at Amiens, by train in the evening, and then we can make that our head-quarters, and penetrate further from there."

"I should love that, but could we arrange it in the time?"

"Of course! Only get your Aunt to consent tonight, and my servant will make all the arrangements."

"Auntie was only saying this afternoon that we must see the battlefields, but it was Château-Thierry which interested her."

"There is nothing to see there, all the traces have gone. I want to show you where the real devastations are. They say the flowers now have grown up and covered everything with a mantle, but there are some grim reminders left sticking through!"

"I'm crazy to see a trench and a dug-out. You were at the war?"

"All the time. Well, we must find you one, if there are any left which are safe to go down. Now, let's make all our plans."

He was gay and friendly, and not once mocking or insulting. They settled everything of how they would proceed.

Laline should start with him in the morning, and the others should go by train to Amiens and they would all meet by dinner-time that night, and start a regular exploration the following day in motors from there.

The Whitmores, who were at the Crillon, would be sure to want to come with them. They should be telephoned early in the morning, in time to get the whole lot off by the twelve-o'clock train.

However much Jack might resent Laline's going alone with David in the two-seater, she knew she could smooth him down. He was so accustomed to stand any amount of her caprices that he would help her to make her Aunt fall in with their plans.

So, thoroughly satisfied with the prospect ahead, David at last took Laline back into the ball-room, to find Mrs Greening.

While they had been arranging, he had not digressed into the realm of flirtation again. There would be ample time on the morrow, and he had other business on hand tonight, but as they crossed the hall he whispered:

"Good-night, honey! Remember, you are never going to be cross with me again, and are going to belong to me tomorrow for the entire day."

Laline did not answer, but her eyes shone.

Mrs Greening was all smiles when the proposition was put before her, and she agreed to everything. Jack's face was rather thunderous, but his was always "Hobson's choice."

Then Major Lamont left them, and for the rest of the evening Laline saw him deep in conversation with the Royal party, and the French Ministers, and yes, Mrs Hamilton, of whom she now had heard, and even though she had the thought of "belonging to him for an entire day" ahead of her, she could not keep back her jealousy.

Why was he so important, anyway? Why did everyone make such a fuss of him? But the realisation of a man's worldly prestige has never yet left women unaffected. So Laline got into her bed that night, more in love, and more impressed with David's value, then ever before.

*   *   *

At eight o'clock the next morning Laline was awakened by the telephone; Celestine had just entered her room and answered it.

"*Monsieur le* Major," she said, and handed the instrument to her mistress, who seized it eagerly.

"Are you awake?" The voice was deep and rather masterful.

"Yes . . ."

"Say, can you be ready by nine-thirty? The morning's too glorious to let it waste."

"Y-yes."

"That means that you aren't up. Do you want me to come and hustle you?"

"What's the matter that you are in such a hurry?"

"The morning, and you."

"I'll be ready if you really want to start so soon. But we'll get there long before Auntie and Jack . . . and the Whitmores haven't even been telephoned yet!"

"Tell your maid to fix all that, and you come with me. Fergusson, my man, is making all the arrangements at Amiens, and he can tell them after we have left."

"All right."

"Honey?"

"Well . . . ?"

"At nine-thirty at the Vendome door—and then don't you forget you're mine for today!"

Laline lay back in her bed, quivering all over. His for today! Yet last night he had been most of the time with Mrs Hamilton.

"Celli, *vite! Vite!* I must be prettier than you've ever made me!"

The maid beamed, and even if disapproval was in her heart, it was difficult for her to resist her loved lamb's joyousness!

David, meanwhile, had dressed and was down examining the motor.

It was a Voison, one of the very newest make, and he knew they would spin along at sixty miles an hour. The Ambassador had said to him just before they had bidden each other good-night:

"You'll have a stiff enough two months, Lamont, so have a good time in your six days! You've got about a sixty-forty chance of getting out without a scratch, boy, or even with your life."

Well, whatever was coming, there should be six days of joy!

He would hold himself as well as he could without spoiling pleasure. And after all, Laline Lester was no debutante from a convent, but most certainly knew every card of the game of flirtation!

She had selected the most ravishing costume of her favourite blue, and no Dresden-china figure ever looked more dainty and appetising than she did, when only about ten minutes late she came down into the Ritz hall.

Her Aunt, Mrs Greening, had been cajoled into agreeing to everything. They would all meet at the Hôtel du Rhin at Amiens for dinner at eight o'clock, and now it looked as though some perfectly divine hours lay ahead of them!

David Lamont came forward to greet her and held her hand. He was gay and not sentimental at this stage.

"You look stunning!"

"You like me?"

"I just want to eat you up!"

Then they got into the car. Laline was settled, the wind-screen arranged, and off they went.

They were in the open country, which was not particularly beautiful, but the green, tilled fields and the gorgeous sun and blue sky made it lovely.

"Tell me what you did in the war. . . ."

"I was attached to the English until we came in."

"And . . . you fought . . . and killed people?"

"I expect so!"

"That must feel odd."

"There is something in all of us which makes a fight, when it comes really to close quarters, jolly exciting; you can think it as brutal as you will."

"And Jack killed men too?"

"Why certainly." David's eyes grew reflective. He remembered one occasion when Jack had used a bayonet with remarkable success!

"Isn't it a mercy it is all over," Laline remarked. "And of course there can never be another war."

"I am not so sure of that. There will always be wars until we have a new religion."

Any other man whom Laline had ever met would by now have been deep in a flirtatious conversation with her, but here they had been driving for what seemed hours, and Major Lamont was still abstract.

What did he mean by saying that she should belong to him for that day, if he was only going to talk about things she could just as well have discussed with Judge Whitmore? Underneath, she had an unrestful sense of insecurity.

She thought of Mrs Hamilton, and at last she blurted out:

"I thought the lady you danced the quadrille with was very pretty."

David turned and looked at her. He understood perfectly, and the flicker of a smile came onto his face. He was immensely attracted. So much so that he had been deliberately ordinary so as not to go ahead too fast.

For he had no illusions, and knew that once they began to talk of each other and their feelings it would be difficult to make the even terms of flirtation last for the trip. And after flirtation, what? He did not want to flounder into an abyss.

"Yes, she is," he said, answering Laline's remark; "and awfully charming. She's a widow. Attractive things, widows!"

Laline's cheeks burnt; she felt very ruffled and very jealous.

"She is an old friend, I suppose?"

He had no intention of gratifying her curiosity.

"Not so very old."

"There are some people one gets to know very well in a short time. I thought you were probably infantile playmates!"

David laughed outright.

"I wish we had been!"

"Are you as fresh with her as you are with me?"

"I am never 'fresh' with any lady."

"Then I can't be a lady, because never before in my life has anyone ever been so fresh with me as you always are!"

"You are a darling little girl, and now you are getting mad with me. What for? I've been as good as a schoolmaster and as meek as a lamb ever since we started."

There was a laugh in his bold eyes, and Laline's grey ones flashed at him.

"You could never be a lamb, you're always a fierce wolf, and the woolly skin doesn't disguise you in the slightest!"

"Do you like lambs best, then?"

"No."

"Then what is there to it? If you are starting out to quarrel with me, there is only one way of stopping it."

"And that is . . . ?"

"I'll park the car when we get to this wooded corner and kiss you back to being kind to me!"

Even though Laline resented his tone of authority, a sense of joy filled her.

They had got back onto her own ground again, one of fencing over personal emotions, so she was quite at home.

"I never heard of such conceit! You imagine that that would make me kind to you. Why, it would only make me hate you all the more!"

"You hate me already, then?"

His tone was full of mock anxiety. He knew very well that hate was not what was holding her.

"You don't believe I do," she said, and pouted a little, angrily. "Well, I'll show you!"

They had come to a delicious wood not a great distance from Beauvais. He slowed down the car and finally stopped.

"Now you're going to show me how you hate me!"

"How?"

"Why, you will want to get out and be left behind; no one likes to travel in a two-seater with a person they hate!"

Laline did not stir.

"I am waiting for you to get out . . . but, of course, how rude of me! You want me to help you!" And he sprang down at his side and came round to her door.

She rose in a rage, and as she stepped forward he took her in his arms.

"Stupid, naughty little darling!" he murmured, as he fondly kissed her red lips!

Laline was incensed and yet wildly emotional. That same feeling of powerlessness came over her. She was insulted, and yet she could not fight, for the kiss intoxicated her.

"Oh . . . please!" she said, gasping, and then she burst into tears!

He held her to him tenderly, and the triumph and the daring went out of his eyes and they softened like night sky when it is beginning to herald dawn.

"Sweetheart, don't cry. I am a brute, I always was, and I should not have teased you. Forgive me, and let's be friends, and I'll promise I won't kiss you again unless you ask me to!"

Laline sobbed for a minute, held close to his heart, and then she pulled herself together.

"It's your insolence. One minute as if you hardly knew me . . . and the next . . ."

"Where I want you to want to be!"

And he rubbed his cheek against hers, but he did not kiss her again.

She gave little shuddering sobs like a child.

"You are the rudest man . . . I've . . . ever met."

"And you are quite sure you hate me?"

She had mastered herself sufficiently now to realise that it was better to answer lightly:

"I shan't tell you . . . because I don't want to be left behind . . . even in a green wood! There might be many bears there . . . and it is better to go on with one!"

And she smiled, but there were two big teardrops upon her bewitching, brown curly eyelashes, and her sweet young mouth still quivered.

David Lamont felt the strongest emotion he had perhaps ever felt in his life. Was he going to fall really in love with this beautiful spoilt heiress, after all?

His eyes blazed, and Laline saw them and rejoiced.

"Honey!" he said a little hoarsely. Then he picked her up and put her in the car again.

"Say you've forgiven me and that we are friends," he pleaded before starting. "I'll talk nothing but the sagest sense until we get to Amiens!"

"I've got to say whatever you like . . . I'm under duress."

"Say, 'I've forgiven you, I don't hate you at all, David!' "

A dimple showed in her left cheek, and she cast her eyes down. Then she repeated the words rather babyishly. She knew she was attracting him now, and she lingered with a little gasp over his name, "Dav-id."

"Darling!" he whispered, and started the car.

Then with the greatest intelligence he laid himself out to amuse and interest her.

He told her the history of all this country, and how she was to notice the beauty of the Beauvais Hôtel de Ville, and how they could stop at the Cathedral on their way back, because he wanted to get to Amiens at about one o'clock, and have luncheon, and get well away into the wilds by the early afternoon.

He was gentle and quite chivalrous. Laline had nothing to complain of, but when they stopped for a moment in front of the Beauvais Town Hall, her heart sank again.

She knew that she would rather that he were insolent than that he should be so respectful and . . . cold!

*　　*　　*

"Notice the immense dignity and sense of proportion in this architecture," David said, as they looked up at the noble façade of the Beauvais Town Hall, standing there like a great aristocrat among its humbler neighbours in the square.

"I've a feeling I want to stay over here a long time," she announced at last. "It's got atmosphere."

"Of course it has. Just think of the hundreds of years of tradition that are hanging round everything. Why, you're bound to feel different. But just think of the wonderful chance we have in our country to create our atmosphere as we like. We need not have any of their old prejudices to hamper us."

"I suppose we are too much in a hurry to think about it . . . and so we leave no mark. . . ."

"That's it, everyone is in a hurry. But it is because we have so much energy, we want to get on, get somewhere."

"What do you do in life?"

Her voice had a note of timidity in it. She had a sort of feeling that Major Lamont would not answer anything that he did not want to.

"I do what I *must,* part of the time, but I hope I shall soon be free to do what I *can!*"

He was being abstract again, when what she wanted was concrete information.

"Are you going to stay long on this side?" She was determined now to find out!

He turned and looked down at her; the quaint tenaciousness of women amused him.

"Just as long as I want," he said, and she saw the whimsical smile in his eyes, and it angered her.

She had the feeling that she was losing ground, and not attracting him as much as she felt that she had been doing some while back. And with every fresh uncertainty about him she fell more and more in love.

By the time they had reached Amiens, David was saying to himself that he was sorry he had told her he would not kiss her again until she asked him, because he was beginning to have an insane desire to kiss her all the time!

It must be his business to *make* her ask him. So he became gentle and tender and considerate, and as they drew up at the door of the Hôtel du Rhin, Laline was throbbing with delicious emotion.

They found that the rooms had been telegraphed for by Fergusson, and they were expected.

Laline discovered that hers was on the first floor. It looked out onto the garden and the monster plane tree.

When she glanced at herself in the mirror over the mantelpiece, she saw her own shining eyes and her glowing cheeks, and she wondered what was the difference in them, for there was a difference in her whole expression!

Meanwhile, Major Lamont, below in the restaurant, was ordering their luncheon. He was a past master at this sort of thing. He instinctively guessed what Laline might like, and everything was ready for her: the Sauterne was on ice, and the hors d'oeuvres were waiting.

He sauntered into the hall where the staircase was and met her coming down the steps.

"The waiters will think we are a honeymoon couple, and so they'll be awfully sympathetic," he said, laughing. "But so we are, for today!"

They were so gay! Laline, now that he was kind and nice to her, blossomed forth into wonderful sweetness, and David began to look forward to the afternoon, when they should be alone again in the open country.

Each was thinking of the other. He was saying to himself that in his whole life, in no country had he ever seen so pretty a girl as Laline. No one more delectable—more adorable. Yes, when he came back he must teach her to love, really to love!

Their lunch was so gay.

David made her hurry over it. Supposing Mrs Greening and the rest of the party had caught the twelve-o'clock train instead of the three-fifty? They might be arriving upon them, and in some way spoil their afternoon. So he was anxious for them to be safely off again with Laline before this could possibly occur.

It was one of the most glorious days of the whole year, not a cloud, and the air was fresh and warm and balmy.

Laline was soon tucked in again, and they were rolling along out of the town, past the descent to the station, and so on to the road which would bring them to Albert.

"Everything is so green now," David said; "it is hard for you to realise what this looked like when we were here, but soon we shall come to parts where you can still see the wretched, burnt stumps of trees."

Then gradually they came upon signs of destruction, and the poor miserable little shelters which had been erected among the battered homes.

As they came to one heap of barbed wire and old iron, Laline cried:

"Why, there is a bedstead! Look! You know that makes me feel the reality of all the horror more than anything else!"

David's face was grave now. Every step contained memories for him. And so through ruined villages and pathetic stumps of trees, half-hidden in the young fresh green, they came at last to Albert, and saw the ruin of the Church where the Virgin and Child had been displayed for so long, until finally destroyed by the advance in 1918.

"Oh! And to think that I laughed and danced through it all, and only played at war work! Of course—of course we never understood!"

"That's it," said David, and there was a mist in his eyes. "Dear France!"

Chapter
Four

They did not get out of the car, and soon they were on the main road again.

"We must come back here with the rest of the party tomorrow, but I just wish to get you to my own little corner, in case Jack might want to show it to you also. I must be the first."

Laline glanced up at him slyly.

"In everything?"

"Yes, in everything that's good. First with the person I love, and first in my work."

"How I wonder who the person you love is."

David's voice was thoughtful as he said:

"Do you know, I too have been wondering that lately."

"She would have to be a meek, spiritless thing."

"Oh, no, she would not, but she'd have to be worthwhile in character, and not just pretty trash!"

"Do you often meet women who are not just pretty trash?" Laline pouted.

"No, frankly, I don't; and when I do, they are generally married to another fellow."

"I suppose you've seen a great deal of the world?"

"Probably."

Laline looked at him, at his jet-black eyes flashing with enthusiasm, his finely cut face like that on some old Roman coin.

A feeling of adoration swept her. Oh! how wonderful to have such a man to love her, and yes, to teach her to be vast and not paltry by his side!

Suddenly she felt how mean and small her aims had been with him! Just to attract him so that he should be bound in the usual chains men were in, in regard to her. A conquest for her own vanity!

But love was clearing her vision. David appealed to something in her soul. He filled her now with the desire to raise herself to be noble, to be *worthy* of him!

David was quite unconcerned about what anyone thought of him; his whole force was concentrated upon earning his own self-respect.

He was brought back to consciousness of her by her little hand, which touched his arm, and looking down he saw a small flower of a face and two soft grey eyes looking up at him with a new expression in them.

A wave of emotion swept through him. He clasped the hand and drew it to his lips and kissed it.

"Dear little honey," he said, "this is in homage, not what you call my 'usual insolence.' "

"No, but it is possessive all the same."

"Well, don't you belong to me, for today?"

"I suppose so. . . ."

Thrills were running through Laline, for "belonging" implied so many divine things.

A mile or two after they had crossed the iron

girder bridge, where the old one had been blown up, David stopped. They had come to a tiny group of houses rather off the main road, with the usual café of boards, cheek by jowl with complete destruction.

Far away to the left, but in front of them, a vast countryside of devastation met their view. In 1921 it had not been all tilled, and deep shell holes and skeletons of trees could still be seen in many places.

"In case we are hungry, do let us buy some chocolate at that little café. I meant to bring some; and I want to see the inside of one of those queer sheds," Laline said.

So they got out of the car and entered the café. A dear old French peasant kept it, who welcomed them with the usual graciousness of his class.

"Chocolate? *Mais oui, certainement!*"

A comely daughter made her appearance, a girl of fifteen or sixteen, whose souvenir of the war was not so tragic as that of her elders. She admired Laline greatly.

"Are there any dug-outs left, to your knowledge?" David asked of the old man.

Not just here, the man told them, but some miles further on towards Gommecourt, if they struck north, there might be; they were stay-at-home people and did not wander far. So contentment and cheerfulness was in this wretched place, and Laline was deeply struck by it.

After a while the road became a mere track and then ceased altogether, and the broken corner of what might have been a Church wall met their view. They had to halt. They were now miles from any human habitation, even the merest board hut.

A battered iron crucifix hung obliquely from a

bent iron pole, all that was left of what had been a shrine. And before it, when they could see behind the corner, there knelt an old, old priest in shabby cassock.

David took off his cap, and said in French:

"Reverend Father, can you inform me whether we are near a village, which was afterwards wiped out, called Etticourt?"

The old man turned to them, and looked at them rather dazedly for a moment.

"You are standing upon part of the outlying ruins of it now," he answered. "This was my Church, that heap of stones over by that trench!"

His mild and saintly eyes gazed at them benevolently, as he pointed to the north. They talked to him for a while.

Yes, the famous German dug-outs were but a quarter of a mile from here, across the fields. No, they had not all fallen in. The salvage men had passed long ago, but they had left the dug-outs undisturbed because the old priest sheltered there.

"One is my hermitage, where I go to pray," he said in a quavering voice.

The rest were in bad condition, and he had heard the last time someone had passed this way, about a week ago, that soon all were going to be filled in, and the steam tractors were coming by August.

They could see that his poor old mind was wandering. His emaciated frame was feeble to a degree. The worn black cassock hung upon it, but he was clean and shaven.

Could he lead them to the dug-outs? David asked courteously. It would be so very kind, as otherwise they might wander aimlessly when once they left the car.

The old priest pointed to the north, across a comparatively smooth bit of ground.

"You could drive over that, *Monsieur,* and then we must walk. I will show you."

They thanked him heartily, but could they give him all that trouble if it was far?

"I will drive *Mademoiselle* to that line of stumps and come back and fetch you, Reverend Father," David said.

The ancient priest bowed with old-world politeness and they went on.

When Laline was left alone for the few minutes when they crossed the smooth ground, she looked round her. What an awful place, so lonely, so isolated.

Nothing could be more melancholy even in the brilliant sun. There were deep shell holes all round, and a hundred yards further on she could see the beginning of a trench facing the stumps of what had been a wood.

The exquisite May sunshine seemed to mock the cruel souvenirs; an ammunition waggon still lay on its side, and what was that horrible-looking monster?

Why, it was a tank! And then David arrived with the priest.

"Yes, this is the place!" he cried delightedly. "What astonishing luck to find it after all this time."

He backed the car onto more firm ground, by a mound, and they left it there, and came on.

They followed the priest respectfully as he led the way towards the trench.

"We took it in a hand-to-hand fight through the wood,'" David told Laline, "and then we had a regular picnic in their dug-outs that night, and the

hell of a tussle in the counter-attack next morning. Then my boss got track of me, and I was
hauled back to my work at H.Q. just when we had
retaken it. It was a glorious adventure."

"You were not supposed to be fighting, then.
What were you doing?"

"Well, I had rather important work, but just
at the moment I had no business there."

They had reached the tank by then. Laline
was full of interest.

"May we stop for a moment, Reverend Father?" David asked. "Miss Lester wants to make
the acquaintance of this prehistoric monster."

The priest hardly seemed to understand. He
looked vaguely over their heads.

"There is a spring by that stone," he said, "if
you are wanting water. I will bring it from there."

Laline was enchanted with the tank. She must
climb up and get into it, she said, but David
would not let her.

"It is full of rust and filth. It will spoil your
lovely suit. Besides, our charming old host looks
as if he wants us to come on."

So, reluctantly she let herself be drawn forward.

"I love its dear old face," she said laughing.
"It reminds me somehow of my cat, Mumps, when
he is sleepy and putting his head down. Someday,
Major Lamont, you must be introduced to Mumps!
He's the thing I love best on earth."

"I'd be proud to compete with him. Why,
here we are!"

The priest was striding ahead again now, and
it was wonderful to see the way his feeble limbs
seemed to support him. He climbed down into the
trench apparently without difficulty.

He lodged now in the village of Oieul, about

two miles to the east, he told them, but often he came and spent a day and a night in this one dug-out, because it contained something of his Church, which the Germans had stolen; the little side altar they had used as a buffet, and there was one of the candlesticks with the seven branches, too.

These things made it sacred to him. It would be very tragic for him in August when the authorities would send people to fill it all in. The salvage men who had passed in 1919 had been very considerate and had not disturbed him there, nor in the adjoining one. Both were in good preservation still.

Laline thrilled. She would see a dug-out at last! She had read so much about them.

They walked down the trench, its banks all covered with green grasses and spring flowers. It would be red with poppies later in the year.

And then they came to openings in the highly banked earth, and they could see very steep stair-cases going down into what seemed the bowels of the earth; one or two were only half choked up with mud; the rest looked thoroughly dilapidated. At last one appeared clear, and David paused.

"What if it should be the very hole old Jack and I got into!" he exclaimed enthusiastically, but the priest went on.

He led them to one which he was not quite sure about, for he had not been in it lately; but his own shrine he could vouch for the safety of, and it was the very next.

David paused.

"After all, I don't think I shall let you go down. I'll go myself and see, and tell you about it. It will be awfully dark, and now, when we have all forgotten the war and those sort of things, it seems odd to be burrowing into the earth."

"If you are afraid, I shall go with the Reverend Father alone, then!" And Laline tripped forward to follow the priest.

"Well, let me go first and see if it is fit for you," said David.

"You are a cautious creature! Look, the priest has disappeared, and if he can spend days and nights there, I am sure it won't injure us any."

"Why, of course not, but still I don't want you to go down."

"Then you'd better learn once and for all that I shall do as I please!" And, laughing, she stepped forward.

"So be it! You had better be prepared, though; the laws of the dark are not the same as the day, and . . ." His eyes were full of passionate admiration.

Laline interrupted him gaily:

"You think I am going to *ask* you to kiss me, then . . . ?"

"No. But I may follow dark laws and do so in any case."

"I am not timid; besides, the priest will chaperon me!"

So he gave her his hand, both laughing gaily, and they began to go down the steep steps.

Before they got very far, Laline turned and looked back over her shoulder at the picture framed by the opening they were leaving. A divine peep of blue sky above the waving flowers at the top of the trench.

"Oh! How lovely the light looks! The dear sky!" she cried, and there was a slight catch in her voice.

David held Laline's hand as they descended the steep steps. Below them they could see a faint light which came obliquely from the excavation into which the priest had already disappeared.

At the bottom of the stairs, a pace or two to the right, there was an opening which was blocked up with boards and earth, and after about six feet of passage to the left, they came into the actual dug-out.

The old priest had lit a little taper which flickered unevenly; the altar's large, branch candlestick still contained its seven tall wax candles, which were unlit.

It stood upon a high oaken table that had once been the skeleton of a side altar, and behind it, on the wall, was hung a crucifix, and beneath it there was a vase of spring flowers and a prayer-book. An old Normandy cupboard met their view at the opposite end.

Laline gazed about her, at the earthen roof and the large bits of board supporting it, at the uneven floor.

There was a strange damp smell that seemed to remind her of a root house in her grandfather's garden, where the potatoes were kept in the winter.

And to think that David had called this "a regular palace," this terrible place of mud and darkness.

Certainly things were relative. And men had lived here—and died here, her thoughts added with a shudder; and she had been safe in America, and not really very worried about it at all.

She crept closer to David's side. Somehow, she felt that she wanted to be near to him. He was by now at the other end of the room.

Excavated in the side of the wall along which the short passage to the staircase opened, so that those sleeping there could get the most air, there were two tiers of bunks, as in a ship, four in all. They had board supports up to the earthen roof.

Beyond the altar, a doorway could be seen with a piece of sacking as a kind of curtain.

Besides all this, there was an old armchair with one broken leg mended by a bit of wood nailed on. It was a relic of the Empress Eugénie's time, and had originally been covered with bright blue satin damask and edged with a deep fringe.

A sofa of the same period was beyond the altar. They had been stolen from the neighbouring Château.

In the centre of the floor, a rude wooden table, made of boards, still stood on its three legs.

It seemed strangely cold after the May sunshine of the upper world.

But nothing daunted Laline's spirit now that the first feelings of weirdness had worn off. Never had she been more gay. She peered about everywhere, and wanted to try on a German helmet which the priest had collected with some bayonets and one or two old trench spades.

The dim light from the entrance was making things clearer after a time.

The old man stood back and watched her. He had handed her his taper. David had got out his torch. He had put in a new refill that very morning, and it was the strongest one of its kind. He flashed it about everywhere.

"You really sleep here sometimes, Father?" Laline asked, unbelievingly, and she was almost aghast when the priest assured her he did so.

"I spent Réveillon and the last day of the old year in meditation, and Good Friday and the Festival of Easter. This is my Church."

He went now to the cupboard and opened the door.

"See, here is my store of candles, my daughter, and my other little necessary things, a jar of water fetched from the spring, and a cup and platter."

"Why, it's quite a home!" Laline laughed.

"All that is left to some of us, alas! All in this trench were like this, the best dug-outs you could find. I had often sat on that chair when I went to visit *Monsieur le Marquis*. The Château of Etticourt was famous for its splendour and its hospitality—"

David interrupted here:

"I believe that's the very chair I remember, but . . ." and he put his hand to his forehead as if trying to recollect, "this is certainly not the dug-out my friend and I were in. . . ."

"No, *Monsieur,* probably not. I brought that chair from the one through the opening. I did not venture further than just by the door, because one never can tell, *Monsieur,* as *Monsieur* knows, and there was a biscuit box on the floor."

There seemed to be some mystery here, and Laline's feminine brain was instantly intrigued. What could be peculiar about a biscuit box?

"You should have let the salvage corps clean it all up, Father," David said. "I can't think why they let you alone."

Then the priest explained how he had pleaded and implored that they would touch nothing just in this one spot, and how he had been able to influence the Commandant not to disturb him in these dug-outs, and two there were, which led from this staircase.

David flashed the torch on the chair. Yes, it certainly was his old friend!

"I don't know why it made us laugh so much," he told Laline. "Perhaps we were so dog-tired that we were silly, but to see her there in the mud and filth after we had been wading in blood and carnage, with her blue satin and fringe, seemed so comic."

"The sofa looks awfully grand, too!" Laline laughed. "Was 'she' also in your 'palace'?"

"No. She must always have been here, but somehow I feel that the one we were in was through that opening. I know it was at the right of the stairs as we came down, and the priest said he took the chair from there."

"The door we saw filled in," Laline suggested. "Oh! Do let's go through the curtain and see it!"

At this moment the priest spoke again, and David went back to him out of courtesy; so Laline, beyond the ray of the torch, and carrying her own taper, went forward alone and lifted the sacking *portière*.

She was so interested to explore the actual place where Major Lamont had been. Nothing dangerous or unknown had ever touched her sheltered life.

The war had been a nightmare to read about in the papers, but it had had no more real effect upon her than a stage play. That it was unwise to take a step here unguided never entered her golden head.

David's torch was so powerful that it obscured everything beyond its ray, and he did not see where Laline was going until he swung the disk round that way, and then with a note of alarm, when he saw that she had gone beyond the curtain, he called out:

"Don't stir a step, Miss Lester. You must not go in there alone."

"Do you think I am afraid of the 'laws of the dark'?" she said, laughing, back at him. "You ought to come and see—this one is not half so grand!"

He strode towards the opening, some strange feeling of fear in his heart, but before he could cover the three paces which separated him from the doorway, a deafening explosion occurred, and a human body was flung against him with violence, and they both fell to the floor, stunned.

After some confused moments, sense came back to him in the choking air. His torch flamed on the floor some distance from him, and by its light he saw that it was Laline who lay there.

Was she dead? Oh, God! His mind came back more fully now, and he went and picked up the torch and flashed it upon the slender body there on the ground.

No, she was not dead. She sat up and looked at him with dazed, agonised eyes, and then she shrieked aloud:

"I stumbled against the biscuit box! Oh! What has happened? Are we buried alive?"

The altar and the crucifix had fallen with the bursting of the wall, and lay there under loose earth, and the head of the poor old priest could be seen obtruding from the heap of debris. He was moaning and his eyes stared wide.

David's numbed senses took in with a ghastly shudder that the passage to the staircase had gone. Laline was right: they were buried alive.

Buried alive in a dug-out! In a lonely place far from the habitations of men, where, if help should ever come from outside, it might not come in time.

The whole horror of the situation made his heart stop beating for a second, but he did not lose his nerve. He put the torch on the table, which he set on its legs again.

He bent and lifted Laline in his arms. She gazed at him in frozen terror; then she gave a great cry.

He carried her to the sofa and laid her down; it was usable and still stood against the opposite wall.

"Oh! Tell me what has happened!" she cried wildly. "I am suffocating. Shall we all die? Don't leave me!"

"I must help the old priest," David said tenderly. "Lie here. Do not be frightened, dear little girl."

But she clung to him, crazy with fear.

Then, when she saw the priest, her frenzied grip on his arms relaxed and she fell back on the couch.

The earth was only loosely heaped over the old man, and David was soon able to uncover him and help him to his feet. He was unhurt, he said, though he moaned, unconsciously, between his words.

David led him to the blue satin-covered chair, into which he subsided for a second, then he started up.

His crucifix and his candlestick—where were they?

The crucifix was still among the debris, but the candlestick was at the other side of the room, apparently undamaged, although the candles were strewn about on the earthen floor.

David found his match-box, and picking up two, he lit them, and now they could see a little more.

Half of the wall leading into the adjoining compartment was down, so that the space was now twice as large.

The smoke was clearing away mysteriously.

Where to? That he must discover, for perhaps in that direction lay deliverance.

The suffocating smell made them all sick and giddy, but even so, David knew instantly that it must have been but a very small bomb, or they would have been blown to pieces.

The earthen wall between the compartments had saved them from the greater part of the shock, and by some miracle Laline had been flung back through the door.

The sacking which had served for a curtain lay close to the sofa now.

An agony of terror was in her eyes when David came back to her. Her face was white, and there was a smear of blood on one cheek, where she had been scratched. He wiped it off very gently with his handkerchief.

She clung to him piteously, and pointed to the heap of earth where the passage to the staircase had been.

"Oh! Save me! Save me! I don't want to die! We are buried alive; we shall suffocate or starve!"

He held her to him with infinite tenderness, as though she were a child.

"Laline, try not to be so frightened. Darling, there is sure to be another way out. Don't tremble so."

And the firmness in his tone reassured her, and brought her more to herself.

David held her close in his arms and smoothed her hair. Her hat had gone. Then he tried to brush the earth from her clothes; it was fortunately very dry. She fell to sobbing now more quietly, and then the priest spoke:

"It is the will of God, my children." His voice sounded far away.

This terrified Laline. The will of God that they

were to die! Oh! Why had she gone through the sacking curtain and laughed at David when he had told her to come back?

She had stumbled against something, and then had come that crash, that horrible crash.

She tried hard to collect her senses and to control herself, but panic was seizing her.

"Save me! Save me! I won't . . . I won't die!"

"Courage, my child," the priest murmured again. "Control this unseemly terror and let us go into God's presence with peace and calm."

He had touched some part of Laline's pride. She flung herself upon her knees before the old man and buried her face in her hands.

"Oh, Father," she whispered brokenly, "help me to be brave! But life is so beautiful, I do not want to leave it!"

The sight of Laline as she knelt by the priest wrung David's heart. How could he save her? He lit one of the candles and took it with him to explore the other compartment.

The full awfulness of the situation was growing upon him now that the first shock was subsiding. But the nerves of the man were controlled by his iron will, and now a rage within himself was holding him.

How had he been such a fool as to risk going down any dug-out which was three years old? He, who had to "carry a message to Garcia" at the end of his six days' leave! This was a sorry finish to the first of the days. And it was all because he had been led away by his desire to please a girl.

Here they were, trapped in the earth, like weasels, with only the slenderest chance of life, and not only he, but she. He held his breath with the pain of the thought. Laline, too, might have to die.

The force of the explosion had been at right angles, and had blown in the whole of the wall which he knew divided the dug-out from the staircase passage.

It might be that it was only that which was down, and the staircase might possibly be clear, if he could dig through to it. He remembered the old trench spades which the priest had shown them.

Then he began to hold the lighted candle in different places, to see where the air was coming from, for the smoke was nearly gone—so, obviously, there must be some outlet to the upper world. He would find it.

Yes, the draught came from the floor in the northern corner, and if this was the dug-out that he had been in with Jack, there was a second excavation below, and he fancied its opening had been in that very place.

Yes, there was the hole now; half closed in by a board on top of it, and sprinkled with the earth from the explosion, it could easily escape view.

It only took him a moment to dislodge the board, and then he could see below. The grim-looking, steep ladder was rotten and broken. But the rush of air gave him hope.

He paused for a moment and thought. If he attempted to climb down there now, he might fall, and become disabled, and then the chance of life for all three of them would be gone.

It might be better first to try to dig through to the place where the staircase ought to be.

Had he been alone, he would not have hesitated for a moment, but would have tried to go down the broken ladder at all costs, there and then.

But the thought of the priest and Laline held him, and made him decide first to try the other plan, but at all costs to get either of the other two to hold the light while he tried to go down.

What were the chances of being saved from outside? They were not great, for there would be absolutely no trace of where they had gone. They had not met anyone after they had bought the chocolates, except the priest, and they had gone right off the main road.

There was the car? Yes! But that might take days to find, having no clue, and then it might be too late.

He went back into the first dug-out to fetch a spade.

Laline was still kneeling by the old priest's side; her hair was all disarranged, some curls of it hanging down.

The priest was talking in French now, telling her of the life to come, and with the whole of her will the poor girl was trying to listen, and to suppress her terror.

And to David there came a new spirit of love for her. There was something so pathetic about her slender outline in the dim light of the one candle, her little hands upraised.

And she would die of starvation, and thirst, unless he could save her.

They would, all three, die!

A sudden, passionate longing for life convulsed him, life and love, and that he might accomplish his duty. The agony that he should fail to "carry the message to Garcia" . . . !

As his eyes rested on Laline, tenderness grew in his heart. He must save her—*his love*. And suddenly he knew that she was indeed *his love!*

All the camouflage with which he had been enveloping his emotions fell from him, and he knew that she mattered to him more than his own life. He loved her really, at last.

He asked her to come and hold the light for him while he looked down the hole once more. And she followed with alacrity.

But when she saw the horrible deep chasm with the broken ladder apparently going down into the bowels of the earth in darkness, a panic seized her. All reserve left her. She could not let him go, perhaps to immediate death, alone!

"David!" she gasped brokenly. "I, I . . . can't bear it . . . you may be killed. I love you . . . I want you. Oh! Let us stay together here till we die . . . or, if you go there, I must go with you."

"Laline!" His voice vibrated with emotion. "My little golden girl!"

He folded her in his arms.

Then their lips met in that divine kiss which means the union of two souls when the dross of material things has fallen from them.

"Heart of me!" David whispered when at last he held her from him.

But then they were startled by a moan from the other room, and they returned there quickly, to find the old priest lying back in the chair, with closed lids, his face ghostly white.

Laline took his thin hands and rubbed them gently, and at last he opened his eyes.

"I am soon going to leave you, my children." His voice quavered. "My work is done, and if it is the Will of God that you follow me, we shall meet again. Peace be with you."

His voice seemed to grow a little stronger and his eyes seemed to burn. It was as though he saw the distant Heaven.

David took a sudden resolve. If it was all hopeless, and they must die, there were still some hours, long hours, before they would begin to feel the frightful pangs of hunger and thirst.

Hours in which love might gild the ghastly prison into Paradise.

His heart began to beat violently. Laline was there, his little love, and if the old priest married them she would be his indeed. His, while life lasted!

And the glory of the thought exalted him, and filled him with courage and purpose.

The priest was surely going to die. No time must be lost through indecision.

He took Laline's hands, and when she saw the look in his eyes, a soft colour flooded her pale cheeks.

"Darling," David said to her, his voice deep with wild passion, "I love you with my whole being, I know it at last. Will you marry me now? Then, if death comes, He will claim us together, as one."

What mattered more to Laline! Ordinary affairs of life had gone into nothingness. A wild exaltation filled her, and all her suppressed desires for love and romance burst their inhibitions.

The price of death seemed nothing to her for such mad joy, to be David's wife! If but for a single day . . . !

"David . . . I am yours," she said softly, her voice breathy. "Let us be married now."

Then they bent over the priest, and David whispered low:

"Father, I love this lady and she loves me; will you give us to each other in the sight of God, before we die?"

The old man sat up erect and looked at them. His eyes then turning with a helpless stare to the place where the altar had been, and he made a faint gesture with his nearly transparent hands.

David understood what he meant, and gave reassuring words; for, to the priest, there could be no true wedding without the sacred accessories.

"We will set the altar again, Father, and then if you give us your blessing, nothing which comes after can matter so much."

"So be it, my son."

Laline then took care of him, while David prepared their Church.

The altar was soon detached from the loose earth, and the crucifix also, and scraping about David found the book of prayers.

Then he collected the scattered candles and set them in the seven-branched candlestick upon the altar, and lit them all, taking the one he had already lit and fastened with their wax grease to the table, plus the one he had held in his hand, to complete the number.

Then he turned to the priest. But as he came towards him, his eye caught the yellow and white of the sprays of spring flowers, which had been flung beyond the heaps of earth. He paused and picked them up and laid them upon the altar, on the vellum-bound book of prayers.

When the old man saw that all was ready, a new spurt of life seemed to enter into him, he started to his feet without assistance, and with David supporting him to where the altar stood, he opened the big, old book.

Laline and David then knelt down on the bare earthen floor.

David took her right hand in his, and drew off a small hoop of diamonds she wore, to keep the huge sapphire her father had given her on her seventeenth birthday in place, as it was too large for her now.

The ceremony began, and it seemed to them, as they knelt there, that a choir of angels was chanting their wedding hymn.

When the ring was on, and all the vows were made, this beautiful bride of death turned two shining, starry eyes upon her husband. In all the days of her sheltered, luxurious life, she had never been so happy as she was now, with starvation, and thirst, staring her in the face.

For Love is a God, and when He comes into his Kingdom, there is no room for fear.

"Mine forever!" David whispered in ecstasy as he bent to give her the first fond nuptial kiss.

But as he spoke the last words of blessing the old priest swayed a little, then staggered and fell forward. And when David caught him in his arms, he knew that he was dead.

He carried the emaciated form into the other compartment and there laid it down, placing his ear to the priest's heart.

Yes, life had fled; the spirit had fulfilled its mission and so passed on.

David folded the thin hands reverently upon the priest's breast, and then he returned to his bride.

She was still kneeling before the altar, her golden head bowed.

"Laline," he said, and his voice trembled with intense feeling, "the Reverend Father has gone to prepare a way for us, if we must die. But nothing matters to us now, only each other. Tell me that you are content!"

Then the radiance of Heaven filled Laline's grey eyes.

"David," she whispered with wild passion, "I would rather die here with you than have life up there with any other man. I love you . . . and I am yours!"

"Soul of me!" was all he answered, and folded her in his arms.

For a few moments of ecstasy David held Laline close, and then he made her lie down and rest, while he went to bury the priest in the other compartment.

He felt no sorrow for the poor old man, for his mission had ended and he deserved his rest. His beloved crucifix should be placed above him.

When after the last spadeful of earth had been thrown over the deeply buried corpse, and the crucifix laid reverently upon it, David went back to Laline, and found her sleeping.

He cleared the place of the fallen earth and began reviewing their resources. Three dozen candles in a box in the cupboard, as well as the seven in the altar candlestick, all but one of which he had carefully extinguished.

The packet of chocolates they had bought in the café, eight squares in all, and a large earthen pitcher of water. He remembered with a pang that his flask of old brandy was in the car, in his overcoat pocket.

He made a calculation.

If they ate one square each a day—each square was as big as a twenty-dollar gold piece—the chocolate would last them for four days, and there were certainly four glasses of water apiece in the pitcher, if not more.

Of candles there would be enough to keep the light continuously for that period, and there was his torch. His box was also full of matches.

Then he put his hand in his pocket, and felt for his revolver, a small six-shooter. Yes, it was loaded.

At the fifth day, if he had not found the way out and no help had come from outside, he would shoot Laline and then himself.

Until then, there was joy and work.

But the thought of joy came uppermost, for he heard his bride stirring, and with giant strides he crossed the floor and knelt beside her.

*   *   *

When all is darkness, neither night nor day makes any difference.

But when, still clasped in each other's arms, the two awoke the next morning, it was seven o'clock, by David's watch. And the second day of his six days' leave had begun.

But though each knew that probable death lay in front of them, their waking thoughts were full of peace and bliss. Something wild was in both their natures, and they had taken mad joy from the anguish of the situation.

For when death threatens full young lives, the spirit of re-creation burns in them more fiercely.

No sheltered bride and groom upon their wedding night in downy silken nest, by the Mediterranean Sea, were ever happier than were these two in the chilly, wretched dug-out.

And now, after divine hours, they awoke upon their couch of straw, with the poor rug over it and the one coarse pillow, and they were full of thoughts of tenderness and love, but horribly hungry.

For their supper had been the one square each of the chocolate, and their wedding wine had been only a tiny glass of water.

David had found some other things besides the candles and the pitcher. A folded blanket and a clean pillow-case. These had seemed as precious wedding gifts, and they had laughed together as they had arranged their bed.

And Laline was sweet and joyous, and said that they were "playing house" like children.

The first day of their marriage must be spent in work, hard digging.

Their dressing could not take much time, for they had neither bath nor hair brush, though David had his pocket comb, and insisted upon being Laline's maid, and combing out her golden curls. This caused him immense pleasure.

"Fairy gold," he called the glistening tresses, and he buried his face in them and kissed them.

"My darling wife, you are so beautiful. How mad and blind I was on that tiresome ship, that I did not know you were mine and claim you at once."

She pouted adorably.

"Arrogance! I knew you belonged to me, though, from the very first moment."

"You were determined to scalp me, little Indian!"

"Yes, in the beginning, just that, but soon ... oh! soon, David ... I had begun to love you ... and ... well ... how much I do now, I just can't say."

He clasped her to him.

"Feel," he said, putting her soft palms against his dark face. "It will require *some* love for me to be able to get by with that, I'm thinking. Sweetheart, how can you care for such a black unshaven brute, you dainty bit of loveliness."

"I like it like that," and she rubbed an exquisite finger on the rough surface; "it looks *strong*."

"Much too strong," he said, laughing. "By tomorrow I shall be a regular ruffian."

"I don't care how you look . . . I don't care if you grow even a horrid beard before we are rescued. You are *my* David . . . and that is all that matters."

When David and Laline were quite ready, they pretended to go to breakfast, and with great ceremony David divided their portion for the day in two halves, one for each.

"Breakfast and supper," he said merrily. "We will have to pretend we are on a diet, and don't eat lunch, or use self-hypnosis to say we are not hungry."

Laline looked a little wistful, so he slipped his arm round her. They had drawn the sofa up to the table.

"You are the bravest, sweetest baby wife a man ever had," he said, and he kissed her. "My own, we will just have to try not to think about it. If I see you suffering it will weaken my nerve."

His attractive voice broke a little.

"And I shan't be able to work. As soon as you have finished that last scrap of chocolate, you must come and help me."

But after an hour David guessed by her silence that she was growing very tired, and his heart was sinking too, for as fast as he dug, more loose earth from the explosion fell in from the top, and he seemed to be making no headway.

"I want you to go and rest now, darling," he said tenderly. "I'll take some measurements, and wake you up again later."

Laline tried to persuade him to let her stay with him, but he was firm. No, she must go to sleep for an hour; he picked her up in his arms, carried her into the other compartment, and laid her down in their bunk.

Then he brought the candle over, and looked at her. She was very pale, and the rough handle of the spade had rubbed the skin off her delicate fingers.

A passionate wave of tenderness swept through David as he kissed them. He must stay with her and pet and soothe her until she sank into forgetfulness. Poor little darling child.

So he pulled up the chair, and sat down beside her, and told her stories, and kissed each eyelid and each curl, and put life into her with his firm-sounding courage and cheerfulness.

And at last, intoxicated by his love words, and his caresses, she felt that it did not very much matter if they were going to die. She was absolutely happy.

But when she was sleeping peacefully, and David went back to his work, his brave heart sank, and a sickening weight grew upon it.

Exhaustion made Laline sleep for several hours. The air was cold and fairly fresh. David could feel it coming up from the hole in the north corner.

He had gone about three feet now, clearing the loose earth right up to the top, where it was solid, and he judged that by four feet more he ought to reach the frame of the blocked-up doorway that they had seen when they came down the staircase.

Then if the logs which supported the side and top of the passage had not fallen in, surely before four days he could dig up the staircase.

If the logs had not fallen in . . . !

That was a disturbing thought.

Of course, given time, he could dig round them; but alone, and without much food, could he accomplish it in four days? Was it possible?

His thoughts went back to Laline.

He loved her now as he had never believed he could possibly love a woman.

Her soul had indeed come through the dross of her education. He thrilled when he thought of her lovely little face, all lit with passion, when she had said she would rather die with him here than have life up there with any other man.

It was five o'clock when Laline awoke, and as she opened her eyes, fear gripped her, as in the first moments after the explosion had taken place. She did not hear David, for he had paused a moment in his work to mop his head.

And the darkness—the one candle was with him—and the silence filled Laline with panic. A scream of terror rent the air, and brought him headlong to her side.

"My darling, what is it? Are you hurt?" he cried with blanching face.

Then shame overcame her. He would despise her for having screamed.

"No, no, dearest." She smiled constrainedly. "I was dreaming. No ... there is nothing. I'm all right."

"I've done a lot now, sweetheart. I am going to rest beside you for a while. Will you hold my hand, darling, while I have a little sleep?"

He lay down beside her on the narrow bed, and she covered him with the blanket. He held and kissed her hand. It was now her turn to lull him to sleep, for he was worn out.

She prayed intently to God to save them, to keep her courage firm, to bring them into the light once more, so that she might give her life to noble things and be her beloved David's helpmate and true wife.

And perhaps angels were listening to her, for presently she too fell off again into the deepest sleep.

Chapter
Five

Laline's Aunt, Mrs Greening, and the Whitmores and Jack Lumley arrived at Amiens by a late-afternoon train on Thursday, getting to the Hôtel du Rhin just in time for dinner.

They were much surprised to hear that Major Lamont and Miss Lester had gone off in the two-seater immediately after lunch and had not returned.

Jack was horribly jealous and felt that he hated his old friend.

Mrs Greening had never seen her niece so interested in any man before. In fact, she had a shrewd suspicion that the "crush" she had was turning into a case of downright love.

When they reached Amiens, and Laline and Major Lamont were absent, the usually complacent Aunt's wrath rose.

When she was ready to go down to dinner at eight o'clock and still there were no signs of them, a dull anger began to burn in her.

Jack was pale with chagrin and jealousy when the party met in the garden outside the large dining-room.

"What can have become of them?" Mrs Whit-more asked.

Nine o'clock came, and then ten, everyone trying to avoid the subject and to act as usual.

But in Mrs Greening's heart there grew the conviction that Laline and David had eloped.

"What do you think can have happened, Jack?" she asked at last. "I am becoming very anxious. What is to be done?"

Jack thought they ought to get a motor at once, and start out along the road to Albert, and make enquiries at the villages to see if anyone had seen them pass.

But it took more than an hour before a car could be procured at that time of the night, and it was nearly twelve when Jack started off alone.

He too began to feel that they had eloped. David was a magnificent driver, and if there had been a bad accident on any road leading out of Amiens, the people of the hotel would have heard of it by now.

When he returned after a fruitless search, at half-past six the next morning, Mrs Greening was pacing her room.

He had not chanced upon the little café where Laline and David had bought the chocolates, for it was far off the main road. One or two drowsy peasants in different villages, angry at being awak-ened from their sleep, said they made no record of cars that passed.

Tourists came pretty often. But one man and his wife did say they believed they had seen a two-seater at about four o'clock that day, with a young man in it, and a young lady in blue. They were going towards Albert. No one had heard of any accident.

Mrs Greening rushed out into the passage as Jack came to her door.

One look at his face confirmed her fears.

"You think that they have eloped?"

Jack was very pale and his jaw was set firm.

"I am afraid I do."

"Where? Where can they possibly have decided to go to?"

"Perhaps on into Belgium."

"Had you any suspicions before, Jack?"

"I have been very uneasy since one night on the ship, but it is awfully unlike old David to do that sort of thing."

"It is not unlike Laline," Mrs Greening snapped. "It is just what she would do to avoid all fuss, and all possible scenes with you."

"I should never make scenes."

His face was full of pain.

"I have been in and out of my bed all night with anxiety."

"Go and lie down now, Mrs Greening. I am going to have a bath and change; later, at breakfast, we will have another consultation."

At Albert, later on that Friday, it was discovered that one or two persons had noticed the pair and the car when they had stopped to look at the ruins of the Church; they had then taken the road towards Lille, it was believed.

Oh yes, they were going along the main road! Then Saturday came, and the distracted party still had had no news.

Celestine and Mrs Greening together were nearly crazy, but both in their hearts believed that elopement was the only solution to the mystery. But why had they not heard by now?

Fergusson had been left in Paris to complete his master's arrangements about equipment for their mission, which was to take them into the unknown at the end of six days, so he knew nothing about all these happenings.

It was not until Sunday, when every available clue had been followed, fruitlessly, that Jack thought of telegraphing to him.

"He would know, if anyone did, what his master would be likely to do," Celestine assured him.

On the Sunday, the fourth day, the police got news of the café; the old couple and the girl had gone on a visit to a married daughter at Calais since the evening of the day they had sold the chocolates, but they returned on Sunday at lunchtime, and, hearing of the hue and cry, they offered their evidence to the police.

The girl told how the young lady was *"belle comme un ange,"* and how the *Monsieur* was so handsome, and they were evidently fiancés, they had no eyes but for each other!

They had asked if there were any dug-outs left, the old man said, and he had told them that maybe there were, towards the Gommecourt district. That was all he knew.

By the time Fergusson arrived at Amiens, Jack and the police had searched Gommecourt. No, no one there had seen a trace of any two-seater.

No dark young man, or beautiful young lady, had entered that village, where just a few shelters had been run up within the last year. The desolate countryside round held no habitations.

When Jack reached the Hôtel du Rhin on Sunday evening, Fergusson was waiting for him.

They had a long consultation together in Jack's room. Fergusson would hear no theory of elopement. His master, he told Jack, had an important appointment with the Ambassador on the coming Tuesday, and not for anything in the world—not

even for the most beautiful lady—would Major Lamont fail to keep it.

"He held no store by lassies," and it was an
accident which had happened, Fergusson would bet
his soul!

"You think so?" Jack said hoarsely, agony in
his heart. "Then, as it all must have occurred four
days ago, and it had poured with rain all night
and the night before, by now they must be dead."

"Dead or alive I'll find my master!"

And dead or alive Jack would find Laline!

*   *   *

On the Saturday morning of the third day's
leave, the married lovers woke very late. Exhaustion and hunger had made them drowsy.

They were clasped in each other's arms, and
David raised himself and moved her so gently onto
the coarse, linen-covered pillow that she did not
wake.

He leaned over and looked at her in the light
of the one candle, now guttering on the table,
which was pulled up close to the bunk.

Her oval face had grown smaller and seemed
very pale. Her babyish brown lashes appeared to
be resting upon violet shadows. There was a pathetic droop of her lips, and her golden curls were
dank.

David uncovered her and put his ear to her
heart. It was beating a little unevenly, and with no
great strength.

Her little hands seemed transparent and felt
damp, and the diamond-hoop wedding ring hung
loose. The big sapphire on the right hand was
gone. It had slipped off in the night from the little
finger, which had grown too small to hold it.

David had found it in the worn old rug, and

put it on the table, and the ray of the candle now hit a facet and a blue radiance seemed to be coming from it.

There was something infinitely solemn in this awakening. It was not joyous like the first morning of their marriage.

But if he had thought he had loved Laline then, he knew now that adoration had entered into his feeling for her.

He had awakened after his two hours' sleep the evening before, and found her in a cramped position beside him; she had not stirred for fear of waking him, and the eyes which looked down into his were as an angel's.

"My sweetest heart!" he had murmured a little brokenly, and clasped her to him.

Then they had supped upon the half-square of chocolate each; then, refreshed from his rest, David had begun work again.

David would not let Laline do any more work, for her hands were blistered from the little she had done the day before.

"You must just sit there and amuse me," he said.

Laline, knowing that it was difficult for him to speak when he was digging so hard, began to sing to him.

She hadn't much voice, but it was nicely trained and very sweet.

"Yes, that is heavenly, my precious little love! Sing to me, it makes work easy!"

And he threw a great spadeful of earth aside with vigour.

She sang all the sentimental jazz songs she had danced to all the winter, and kept time with a slapping of her hands. It kept her warm. And the gaiety of the tunes raised their spirits.

"I do believe that if I keep on, I shall be through by morning, darling!" David said after a while. "And then we will just run for the car!"

"Don't you wonder what the others are doing?" Laline asked, laughing. "Auntie and Celestine will be sure we've bolted to Brussels, because I've always said I would love a runaway wedding. Willmon Dodge often used to implore me to elope with him. Fancy if I had gone!"

David stopped digging for a moment.

"Willmon Dodge!" He looked at her—slender figure, still so neat in the blue frock; at her bewitching little face; and the golden curls, combed out and hanging down her back like a child's now to please him—and a fierce, primitive passion swept him.

His black eyes flashed. Indeed, he looked a ruffian standing there with the spade in his hand, and with his dark, unshaven face bristling with nearly three days' beard!

"David!" exclaimed Laline, surprised. "What is the matter?"

"I'm damned jealous, that's all!"

Some of her old flirtatious mood came back to her. This was simply delicious—David, jealous! It was she who had been jealous before, not he!

"Willmon Dodge is a very nice boy!"

"Just a tango partner! You know, when we get back I shall not stand for any of these fools hanging round!"

"Indeed! I am to be shut up and not allowed to dance, then! I wonder why you go on digging to get out. I'd be safer here!"

Her whole face was sparkling, for she was once more back in her element—teasing a man.

He put down the spade and seized her rather roughly in his arms.

"Look here, young woman," he said. "You're not dealing with one of those mut-heads, remember; your husband knows jolly well how to look after what belongs to him!"

He kissed her with passionate fierceness, his lips almost bruising her soft lips, and the bristles of his moustache scratching her fine skin!

A wild quiver of passion flowed through Laline. How she loved him! How she worshipped his strength! She of course would never want any silly Willmon Dodge worshippers, never any more!

"Oh . . . D-a-vid!" she said, and gasped, when he released her a little. "What a dreadful . . . adorable . . . brute . . . you are!"

"I am glad you said 'adorable'!" And he sat down on the blue satin chair, with her still in his arms, everything forgotten in the passion he was feeling.

"I want to make you adore me always. I am a brute, I know, and I would kill any man who attempted to take you from me!"

Laline felt intoxicated with emotion, and work was forgotten for a time.

*   *   *

David thought of all this as he looked down at Laline that next morning, asleep there on the coarse pillow.

Yes, he would rather die, both of them together, than that any man should ever take her from him! He knew that she loved him utterly, that he was complete lord of her, body and soul. But his peculiar and masterful temperament did not cause him to value her any the less for this knowledge.

That was his way; unlike most men, he loved only when he could rule, and however much physi-

cal charm could have held him for a spell, he
never would really have given his faith or his tenderness without respect for character.

It was when Laline had told him that she
would rather die with him than live with any other
man that the whole force of his emotion had gone
out to her.

Now each hour had made her more dear, as he
discovered fresh sweetness hidden away under the
crust of her stupid upbringing.

She lay there pale and fragile, and in two more
days, if no help came from outside, and he could
not dig through to safety, he must shoot her, and
then shoot himself.

For even now, cruel pangs of hunger were
beginning to torture him. And what would happen
when it came to the last piece of chocolate, the last
sip of water?

What was she suffering, this delicate, exquisite
girl? She had shown no signs of her pains of hunger to him, if she felt them, and they must have
begun to gnaw at her as they had begun to gnaw
at him.

If by chance they ever emerged into life once
more, with what passionate devotion and care he
would repay her for her tenderness!

Then a thought came: she might have a child,
his child! This was too glorious, and sent the blood
coursing through his veins once more, and he bent
down and kissed her mouth.

Her eyes slowly opened, and before she knew
where she was, they suffused with languorous passion for him.

"D-a-vid, I was dreaming that we were on the
ship again . . . but under the stars . . . the last night
. . . when I did not see you. The stars held us in
the light. Oh! How much I love you . . . darling."

The sentence came brokenly, as though some pent-up emotion were escaping.

Then she turned to him and put her arms round his neck, pulling him close.

"David . . . I love you. Near you, I have no more fear. Your lips on my lips. Your heart on my heart. I belong to you. I am yours!"

And so they remained clasped close, without movement, fused in some ecstasy for a long space. The gold of their love was refining in the fire of anguish.

Later, David worked like a beaver, and when their lunch-hour came, hope had begun to spring in his heart. He really believed that in an hour or two he would reach the staircase.

Laline had put on an extra spirit of cheerfulness. She made speculations as to what the others were doing, and to how soon they would find them.

"David," she said, "could we not keep a little more light lit all the time? There are enough candles to last as long . . . as long as we could possibly live . . . even if we burnt four a day. It would be nice if it was lighter . . . wouldn't it, dear?"

"Darling, by all means light three candles in there. And do rest. Sleep passes the time, and then I'll come to you presently with good news."

"I hate to leave you working. David, do you think we might have a cigarette?"

For some unaccountable reason, they had hitherto forgotten that they possessed any.

"I have four in my case," he answered. "I meant to fill it at Amiens, but I was so in love with you that I forgot!"

"And I have six in mine!" She held up a blue case. "Shall we?"

"Let's!"

So he sat on the blue chair and she sat on his knee. Hope was in their hearts. Even with the constant falls of earth from above, which had continually hindered the advance and upset all his hopeful original calculations as to time, he must be through to the staircase in another half-hour.

The cigarettes seemed like whiffs from Paradise. How soothing! How satisfying! David's brain seemed as clear as crystal.

A ray of light struck the diamond monogram on Laline's case.

"Is it not incredible that men go down willingly into the earth to find those! And gold too! I don't think that I shall ever want to see anything which comes out of a mine again; shall you?"

Laline shuddered.

"Never again. It seems that God can only live in the sun, and the blue sky."

"We must be sensible, darling. Come to me and kiss me. We mustn't let our minds get wild."

"David," she whispered; a strange passion, perhaps a memory of some former life, dwelt in her eyes.

"What does death or life or anything else matter? I want to be close to you. I do not want anything between us. I want to feel your skin."

*   *   *

Late at night on that Saturday, David made Laline go to rest without him. He knew that he must work on now, while his strength held out.

So when he had lit three fresh candles, and set them on the table, and had tucked her up and kissed her, he returned into the farther compartment.

Laline had pretended that she was sleepy, so

as not to disturb his mind, and had obediently shut her grey eyes before he left her.

Often she found it so difficult to keep back tears, and she could have cried for the slightest thing, but as her body weakened, so her spirit grew stronger.

Never in all the days of her safe, sheltered past had she been so sweet, and outwardly balanced, as she was now, half-starved, and cold, and with a horrible death threatening close in front of her.

Her one thought was concentrated not on *life* but on what would be the best for David.

She had begun to feel dreadfully hungry at last, and the sick feeling was developing into a gnawing. She found, as she lay with her eyes closed, that she was experiencing a strong temptation to get up and go steal the last square of chocolate, which was portioned for tomorrow—Sunday.

It seemed as though some force stronger than anything she had known was drawing her, drawing her to the cupboard.

She fought it, and a pain began to come into her head, and she fancied that she heard bells ringing. She started up into a sitting position, and listened and listened, but it was only the noise of David's spade.

She could not see him from there, because he was several feet deep in the tunnel he had dug.

A dreadful possibility flashed into her mind. There was that hole in the other compartment, going down into the bowels of the earth. What if awful animals really *did* live there? What if one of them was crouching in the shadows, waiting to spring upon her!

Her teeth chattered, and sweat dripped from

her forehead onto her hand, as she clutched the blanket.

She could not bear it!

She must repeat a poem. She tried and tried to remember one, but nothing would come, only "Gentle Jesus, meek and mild . . ." And "Ho! Ho! And a bottle of rum . . . !"

She must, *must,* get up, and see and meet the creature. Better that than this agony, this agony which was killing her.

She thought she saw a huge monster, but it was only her shadow. No living beast was there to hurt her.

For a second her self-control broke, and she let out a sharp, sudden laugh.

David caught the echo of it in his eight-foot tunnel, and it seemed the most awful sound his ears had ever heard.

What was it and where did it come from? He threw down his spade and rushed back to the living room.

"Oh! David!" Laline cried when she saw his worried face. "I . . . I have had the most ridiculous dream . . . don't bother about me . . . it just made me laugh so. I'll tell you about it, and make you laugh too, darling, when you come to bed. Go on with your work now."

To disabuse his mind of any anxiety for her, she snuggled down beneath the blanket. A part of David's brain knew that she was doing a wonderful thing of courage for him; but even though her words formed a perfectly natural explanation, tears started to his eyes, and his voice was hoarse.

He came over to her and knelt by the bunk.

"My love. My little white soul," he murmured brokenly, and then pulled himself together instantly.

He must *not* give way to any emotion which would unhinge them both.

He looked at his watch lying on the table.

"It is one o'clock," he said rather abruptly, as the thought came to him that the fourth, and last, day of food had begun.

Laline smiled gently at him, and leaning forward kissed his rough, black, unshaven face.

He felt her hair all wet when she was close to him, and he knew that she had been going through agonies of fear.

Something within his heart seemed to grow tight, and then to heave, and tears started to his eyes again. But he controlled himself.

He must not give way now, when hope was with him; he must be nearly through, for even if he had miscalculated the actual spot of the staircase, he was still digging in loose earth and not an old solid mass, so if he struck upwards he would be bound to come out.

He bent down and tucked Laline in again, and kissed her tenderly.

"My darling—my brave, darling wife," he whispered.

Then he left her.

Gradually sleep came to Laline, with dreams of angels holding out their arms, and in her ears there was the sound of sweet music and the soft fluttering of golden wings.

If they got out in a few hours he could still "carry the message to Garcia" on time. And what should he say to Laline? How much could he tell her? Not one word, according to his instructions.

He could only ask her to trust him blindly and promise her that he would return after two months. It would be better for no one to know of the wedding until he could come to claim her. Would she trust him?

But of course she would.

And then they would have to be married over again, for there was no proof they could produce of any ceremony.

The priest was dead. There would be only their word.

David wore no rings. He could not even give his wife that token. Her wedding ring was her own.

Two months was not very long, fortunately. He would be back at the end of July. He might go as far as telling her to write to the Grand Hotel at Rome, so that he could receive her letters on his return journey.

The idea of the mission seemed to help bring into his imagination a certainty of getting out.

He felt sure that just a few more shovelfuls would produce some peep of daylight.

He began to whistle in his eagerness, and the strain of the work seemed light. His thoughts wandered again.

But what was this? His spade struck against the end of a log.

The *end* of a log, not the side of one. He dug obliquely, with frantic energy, his heart beating as if it were in his throat. Then he came to the end of another. . . .

This meant that the explosion had forced the supports of the blocked door outwards. By their angle, he knew that they must now block not only the passage but the narrow entrance to the staircase itself.

And no human being, alone and weak, could dig round the logs, and then through the solid mass of stones and gravel and hardened earth of the untouched natural wall, in time to escape.

He fell forward onto the heap of mould, with a strangled, agonised cry.

"Oh! My God!"

* * *

When David recovered from his despair a little, he stood up on his feet and told himself that he must be a man.

There was one other chance—the lower excavation, from which the air came through.

Some means must be discovered for him to get down there and back.

That was the difficulty—to get back.

Perhaps it would have been wiser to have tried this plan to begin with, he thought, but such speculations and possible regrets availed nothing now.

His motto for all things had always been "action," and he knew he had better put it into practice now.

So he went over to the hole and pulled the short boards away from it, and peered down into the depth. But the candle was no use, so he went into the other compartment to fetch his torch, which he kept carefully in the cupboard.

When he flashed it down into the hole he saw the gleam of water, perhaps over twenty feet beneath, and the rotted ladder did not nearly reach it.

Had the water always been there, or had it come since the last time he had looked? He did not remember having seen any before, and the air seemed fresher, damper, and colder.

All this proved that there must be some opening up into the next dug-out, and so to the outside air.

He must know how deep the water was. He

threw a stone, and by the splash and the bubble that followed he gathered that there were only about six inches of it.

Perhaps it had rained outside and this had run in from above?

He felt overcome. He must sleep for an hour or so. Sleep, like food, restored.

So he crept back to Laline in the bunk and lay down beside her, after extinguishing two of the candles.

She awakened when she felt that he was near, and with a sigh of fondest love slipped into his tired arms.

"David," she whispered, "the angels will come for us, whether it is to take us to them or back to the earth again. I have no more fear. . . ."

He clasped her close to him. He would tell her nothing now of what had happened, and for a few more hours they would sleep in peace.

Chapter
Six

For eighteen hours they slept the heavy sleep of utter exhaustion. The whole of Sunday passed, and it was three o'clock on Monday afternoon, the fifth day of their incarceration, before either one really awakened.

Laline was the first to open her eyes, and she lifted her golden head from David's breast and very gently, with one of her small forefingers, felt the black bristles on his chin and cheeks.

For some reason this touch had the power to bring life into her, for the bristles were so real, so very much as though David and she were living beings.

A man who had a strong growth of black beard couldn't be a spirit, and if she could feel that growth with her finger, and the sensation could produce a thrill in her, she could not be a spirit either, for spirits could not have physical thrills.

No, they were alive, David was there, and he was her *husband*.

He was so exhausted that he never woke despite all her gentle touching, so she could gaze and gaze at him, in the light of the one candle, now only half-an-inch high; he had lit a fresh one at about seven o'clock that morning.

Her head was so light that it seemed to be very large, stretched out as big as one of the heads at a carnival, and full of air. Was it a balloon?

She felt it suddenly. No, it was her own head, just the same shape as usual. Then she reasoned with herself.

"You are becoming silly, Laline Lamont, because you have not had enough to eat."

She began to kiss David's eyelids, and with her soft cheek caress his black-bearded face ... the scratchy feeling was delicious ... so real ... so *real!*

She touched his hair, and his eyebrows, and the lobes of his ears, all as though she were counting marvellous possessions.

David woke at last. He had been dreaming, in that instant near to waking, that he had gone down the blanket rope to the lower dug-out and could not get back again, and he had heard her voice calling to him, and he knew he could not reach her because an unknown beast was strangling him.

The sweat started to form on his forehead, and he struggled, and threw Laline from him so roughly that her head hit the side of the mud wall.

Then he quite awakened and saw her lying there, looking at him, tears gathering in her lashes. And in anguish he bent over her.

"My darling, my sweetheart, I was dreaming a terrible dream. Did I hurt you, my own?"

Laline was crying now, passionate sobs shook her, and tears poured from her eyes. He had thrown her away, he did not love her any more!

He clasped her to him, and kissed and kissed the place where her head had struck the wall. She was not hurt, or even bruised, but the tears were relieving some of the strain.

David was distracted. A thousand times he would rather have died than have hurt her.

"My wee baby," he murmured in a broken voice, fondly caressing her and clasping her limp, fragile body to him, "won't you forgive your brute?"

His voice brought her to herself.

"Everything! I like him to beat me . . . then I know that I am his!"

David realised that all the camouflage of a lifetime was falling from Laline, and the precious little body he was holding to his heart contained a spirit freed from shame.

"Darling," he whispered, making his voice sound as buoyant and cheerful as he could, "I've thought of another splendid plan, though I can't think why it did not come to me before. . . . If you will let me take the blanket and the rug and the pillow-case, and tie them together, I can then easily swing down to the excavation below, where the air comes from, and find the way out."

She gave a short cry and clung to him.

"Then you'll take me too, David. I won't be left alone. If you do not, I will jump down after you."

"No, darling, you will not," he answered a little sternly. "You must obey me, and show me that you are just the bravest darling a man ever had to rely upon. You will come now, when you are dressed, and help me, and you will see for yourself it is quite safe and I can return to you when I have investigated."

The firmness of his tone quieted her fears. She did not protest any more, but let David lift her from the bed and find her shoes for her. This was his daily and nightly task of joy!—to put on, and take off, her tiny grey suede slippers, and kiss her cold little feet.

He teased her about her big toe showing through the hole, to hearten her up, and kissed it especially, and it tickled her and made her laugh so that they became quite gay.

Then he fetched the chocolate and divided it carefully with his knife.

"Only a very small breakfast this morning, sweetheart!" he said, smiling, "but think of the feast we will have, we'll eat the whole lot when I come back!"

Even this minute piece of the sweet stuff and the sip of water brought some comfort. Both their minds became more normal, and David went on to the opening in the floor, carrying his clothes with him, and then he began to make his plans for descending.

He would have to jump three feet straight up in the air to catch the end again from below, and he doubted if by now his strength was sufficient for that.

He must have Laline's frock, there was nothing else for it.

"David!" she cried, a little wildly, when she caught sight of him coming towards her in his scanty clothing. "Dearest, what is it?"

He laughed boyishly. He did indeed look quaint with his unshaven face, well-combed hair, and just his cobwebby under-things.

"I've had to turn the rest of my garments into a rope, darling, and now I have come to ask for your frock. It seems a darned shame to take that lovely blue silk thing from you, though!"

Laline had got it on by now, and was standing there in it. Her face as ethereal as an angel's, her slender figure shrunk and emaciated, and all her gold curls hanging down her back, she might have been a child of twelve years.

David was laughing, so she must laugh too!

"What fun!" she cried with pathetic gaiety, and began at once to pull the woven garment over her head again.

They measured it—dragged to its full length, it would make five feet from the ends of the long sleeves to the bottom of the skirt.

This was splendid!

Then David made her put on his coat over her little crêpe-de-chine, scanty under-garments, and she looked like some lovely little figure in a comic opera as she stood there waiting for him to tell her what to do next.

He took her into the farther compartment, and when she saw the tunnel, which seemed to go so far in, a suspicious look came into her face.

"David . . . did you find it? It . . . was an impossibility. . . ." And she pointed to the entrance where the big mound of earth was.

"And is that why you are going to try this other plan now? And if it fails . . . ?"

He did not speak, he could not. He just folded her into his arms.

She seemed to become deadly cold, and her breath came quickly.

"I'm . . . I'm . . . not afraid, David. We'll go to sleep together."

He could not keep back the tears in his eyes. She had touched his soul.

"God's going to help us not to fail," he whispered hoarsely.

* * *

Fergusson wasted no more time in surmises as he stood there in Jack Lumley's room at Amiens on Sunday night.

"We could send an aeroplane up to see if it could locate the car," he suggested. "I could go now and arrange for one, and have it start at day-break."

Jack found this a good idea. Why had they not thought of it before?

Then a shrewd look came into the Scotsman's sandy-coloured face.

"You would not be knowing of any particular part that Major Lamont might be wanting to show to a lady?" he asked. "I believe, sir, you were with him when he got away from headquarters to enjoy a scrap that time."

"By Jove! Yes!" And Jack bounded to his feet. "There were some dug-outs at a place called Etti-court. He might certainly make for those; they were splendid ones. But the police have been round all those roads and there is no trace of a car. However, we'll try that again. We must start now."

"It is a black, dark night, sir. It would not be any use till dawn. Get some sleep, sir, and I'll see the police at once and make arrangements for the aeroplane to go up, and at three o'clock in the morning I'll call you and we'll start."

"The car must have upset and fallen into a ditch," Jack said.

"Nobody heard an explosion, sir?" Fergusson asked at last.

Jack was startled.

"Why, no! What do you mean? There couldn't be dud shells about now—the salvage men passed in 1919."

"Major Lamont and the young lady might

have gone down a dug-out, sir, and the roof could have fallen in."

This awful suggestion turned both men's faces pale.

Jack saw how his jealous conviction that David and Laline had eloped had obscured his imagination. If he had not felt certain that elopement was the case, he surely would have considered the possibility which Fergusson now put before him.

But if it should be true! The agony of it! Laline, buried alive!

"I cannot wait until the morning," Jack said firmly. "I must start for Etticourt now."

"Very good, sir. I suppose I can get another car, and join you when I've seen about the aeroplane. But you won't do no good until dawn."

They settled their plans. Then it was about midnight, and by two o'clock both Jack Lumley and Fergusson were speeding along towards Albert, with spades and ropes and brandy in the car.

They had left orders for ladders and all other necessaries to follow to Gommecourt with the gendarmes and Judge Whitmore as soon as it was daylight, so as to have everything in readiness for what they might find.

It was raining and miserably chilly. Jack had waited for Fergusson after all, and both had gone to the police about the aeroplane. One should certainly be sent in the morning, and it should fly low over all that part of the country.

When they reached Albert the sky was still inky, but dawn would be there in less than an hour, and Jack's passionate eagerness had to be crushed for that time.

They made for the Gommecourt direction. Etticourt, Jack knew, had been wiped out, and would be difficult to find without some guide. At half-past four, when it had become quite light, they came upon some peasants who gave them some information.

The site of Etticourt was over there to the right, and yes, there were some dug-outs left along by the stumps which had been a wood.

As they turned into the very side track which David and Laline had taken on the Thursday before, they saw an aeroplane circling far in the distance. This comforted them a little.

Jack, who was driving, put on all speed, but they came to the end of the track and to the dilapidated iron crucifix. No road went on.

The rain of the last days would have obliterated any marks of the car across the open space, had there been any, which was very unlikely, as the ground was dry at the time David and Laline had crossed it.

"We'd better go on," said Fergusson, "as far as we can."

The aeroplane was now coming nearer, flying very low.

The airman must discover the car if it was about anywhere at all.

The rain had made the open space impossible to drive across, so the two men got out and walked. They could see the derelict tank in the distance and made for that, but before they could reach it the aeroplane was above them and swooped so low that they could hear the observer's voice shouting in French:

"The car's there, beyond the mound!"

They raced the last hundred yards, and then they came in sight of it, and were soon beside it, and could see David's overcoat and Laline's wrap still in it.

"Oh, God! Fergusson, you must be right!"

They hastened to the trench and climbed down.

There was no sign of anything to guide them. They passed all the dug-outs, with the staircases half fallen in, and at last they came to one where the earth looked as though it might have crumbled more recently than was the case in the others, but the soaking rain made everything look very much the same.

"This is the trench Major Lamont and I took," Jack said, his voice hoarse with the agony he was suffering, "and one of these dug-outs must be the one we were in; the Tommies called them Grosvenor Square. Ours was the seventh staircase from that end, I remember quite well—I was there for days."

"That'll be the one my master took the lady to," Fergusson announced a little breathlessly, and then he began to shout very loud:

"Are you there, anybody?"

"See!" Jack exclaimed, as he went very close to examine the earth of number seven. "There must have been an explosion after all. Look at this biscuit-tin lid—it has been recently blackened!"

The staircase was filled up to the top step, and a log support of a door could be seen sticking out.

He rushed back to number six. This was still quite clear, though the steps were broken away.

"If they are in there, we can get to them through here!" he shouted to Fergusson. There were double excavations, and the ladders went down from each and they joined below.

Then Jack made Fergusson tie the rope they had brought with them firmly round his waist, and himself kept hold of the other end of it, and taking one of the spades he began to go down the stairs, and then he shouted with might and main:

"David, are you down there? David! Laline!"

But he had little hope that any voice would answer him. This was Monday, the beginning of the fifth day since they had been missing.

Without food and water, surely they must be dead.

*   *   *

David jumped down first to investigate, and with a sigh of relief he thought they would be able to get out.

But it was more difficult for him to get back, and when he reached the top he fainted.

Laline shrieked in agony and threw herself beside him.

"David! David! My beloved!"

She kissed him and kissed him despairingly and tried to hold him to her. But his head fell like a leaden weight on her breast. It could not be that he was dead!

Oh, God!

In her anguish for her loved one, all feebleness of her own was forgotten; her spirit had risen beyond the flesh. She laid his dark head down upon the ground again.

His eyes were closed and the heavy, inky lashes rested upon blue shadows, and the part of his face which was uncovered by the growth of black beard looked a greenish olive in the flickering light.

Laline somehow got to her feet and went back into the living-room. She was in control of herself now.

She searched and found the remaining chocolate and the cigarettes and the last glass of water, and she brought them to where David lay.

Then she returned and fetched the altar candlestick, with its seven flaming lights, and put it on the floor near him.

She took his wrist and felt his pulse. There was an almost imperceptible beat.

He was not dead, thank God!

She put the glass of water to his lips and a little stream ran into his mouth.

Then she lit a cigarette and puffed the smoke into his face. His eyelids quivered.

With frantic eagerness she now broke off a corner of the chocolate and forced it between his teeth. He was reviving, and, not conscious of what he was doing, he swallowed the chocolate eagerly.

Then Laline fed him it all, both their portions for the remaining time they could possibly live. Not one thought of self held her. She was ruled by the one passionate urge to save him, her adored one.

David was recovering rapidly. He had unknowingly devoured the sweet stuff ravenously, and now he raised himself and consciousness came back to him, and with it some terrible apprehension of what he had done.

He saw the little figure kneeling beside him with ethereal face and burning eyes looking at him through the smoke and the mist of her hanging golden hair, and he tasted the chocolate in his mouth.

Then he cried aloud in anguish, as the full realisation came to him.

"Laline—Laline—what have you done . . . ?"

And with a great sob he covered his face with his hands. Knowledge of her sacrifice broke his self-control and he shed bitter tears.

She soothed and comforted him like a mother with a child:

"My darling ... my David, you mustn't ... mustn't cry!"

"Oh, my God, Laline, you angel! And I have taken your last chance of food. Oh, the brutish beast that I am!"

Laline felt exalted. It seemed as though nothing mattered now that she saw David sitting up and strong again.

A faint colour came into her waxen cheeks.

"It is much better like this, darling," she told him, "because now you will be stronger and able to save us both. I ... I'm not a bit hungry, and this cigarette was so good. ..."

She laughed softly and kissed him again and again.

David pulled himself together. There was truth in her words, and no time must be lost in remorse or useless grieving. Action was the thing while the new strength was in him.

"Darling child, you are too noble and good, and now we have the hardest task in front of us, but there is daylight at the end of it."

Laline's eyes glowed.

Together they went back into the living-room and collected the few things. Alas! No food now, and only five cigarettes.

They stowed the lapis boxes in the pockets of David's coat, and the matches. Then they took the pitcher and the bed pillow and deposited them next to the hole.

He remembered everything, even the book of prayers.

Then they blew out all seven candles and threw the candlestick down, and they heard it splash in the water. They kept alight only one burning end, which David had scraped off the table.

The table itself was too big to get it through, and it must be left behind, and the sofa also.

Laline suddenly ran back into the dark and left him. He cried to her and seizing the candle end ran after her.

She had gone to the bunk, flung herself on her knees, and was passionately kissing the wooden side.

"Good-bye . . . good-bye!" she cried a little hysterically. "We can never be happier in Heaven than we have been here!"

Then with wrapt face she let David lead her back to the tunnel.

Before he began to swing himself below, David turned to Laline and explained exactly what she would have to do.

He tied the bundle of candles and his matchbox round his waist with the silken belt, as well as his torch and the revolver. She should have light at least to go down into.

Then, seeing that the pockets of his coat, which she still wore, were filled with all the little things, he clasped her in his arms.

"I am sure it is going to come out all right, darling," he said, making his voice sound cheerful. "And even if we can't get out the other side, we have a chance by shouting up for help to where the daylight comes from."

He was feeling so intensely that he feared to give way to any emotion.

Laline was praying silently and did not speak, praying for strength of fingers to untie the knot which fastened the silk jersey to the blanket, praying for courage to drop into the space which seemed so terribly vast, before David could catch her.

He thought about the knot.

"Darling, the only thing which troubles me is that my weight will have pulled the fastening awfully tight between the two things. You must use my pocket-knife if you can't get it undone.

"The jersey comes well through the hole. You, hanging, will be quite five foot eight or ten. I am six foot one, so your jump will not be so very long; but, all the same, I can't bear to leave you alone up here even for these minutes."

They embraced fondly, and then David went down through the opening and arrived safely at the bottom, where he set up the candlestick, which had fortunately only been bent, not broken, by its fall, and he put two of the candles into it and lit them.

Then he placed the candlestick some feet away, and deposited the other things safely in the dry compartment beyond, so that he should be unencumbered when he must catch Laline as she let go of the rope.

The blue satin chair had fallen on its side and was not damaged. It seemed a heavy burden when he lifted it to carry beyond.

"Now throw me the pillow, darling," he called to Laline, "and then the pitcher, and the book of prayers."

She leant over and dropped each thing as he requested. He caught them all and carried them to safety. And then he came back and stretched out his arms.

But panic was suddenly seizing Laline. *She could not face the descent!*

She kept herself from screaming, that was all she could do, but the mad beating of her heart seemed to produce suffocation. Her poor little body shook like a leaf in the wind.

She ran up and down, up and down the compartment. She went quite mad for some moments. Then she heard David's voice calling:

"Laline! Laline! Aren't you coming, darling?"

She stood still.

"David!" she called back to him, and there was a sharp gasp of fear in her tone.

He understood, and his voice grew calm and quiet.

"Courage, my brave-hearted one!"

It steadied her.

"I am coming, David."

He answered cheering words now, and began to whistle gaily one of the jazz tunes which she loved.

She drew up the rope and tried to untie the knot. It was very difficult, as there was no force in her enfeebled fingers, but with the aid of the knife she got it undone at last—it seemed after endless moments.

She bent over the aperture and peered into what seemed the gaping abyss, and she threw the severed portion to David.

He caught it and called:

"Make a knot at the end of the dress, darling, and if your hands slip they will come to it."

He carried the rope to safety, throwing it through the door of the dry compartment.

Laline's very arms trembled, but she obeyed him and then called:

"David . . . are you ready?"

"Yes, darling!"

She grasped the silken rope, plucked all her courage together, and slipped over the side of the hole.

The jerk was such that in her weakness she let go at once, and she hung there, dangling.

It was a moment of frightful anxiety for David,

watching her, but he caught her in his arms, though the impact caused just what he had feared it would, with his strength gone: they both fell flat in the muddy water.

He struggled up and lifted her tenderly. She was shaken and probably bruised, but no grave hurt had resulted. Only she was all wet and shivering.

He carried her through the remaining space and deposited her on the floor of the opening. Even the strain of her light weight seemed immense, and he was panting for breath.

"Go in, darling," he gasped, "and I'll fetch the candlestick."

She got to her feet with difficulty; she was dazed from the fall and the shock of the cold water. In a minute or two they were both safely in the dry compartment.

It seemed like a haven of rest after their adventurous passage to it!

David pointed upward to the opening.

"You can't see the daylight with the candles alight, darling, but it is there all the same. And now, when I have got my breath again, I must begin to try and throw the bar through the hole and make us a new staircase."

The tumultuous emotions which Laline had been through were beginning to make their reaction. She felt very faint and inert. David's voice sounded far away.

The two candles appeared like flaming eyes in the darkness. One of her arms hurt awfully. How could they possibly climb up the rope again? She never could, certainly. Would it not be better to give up trying to escape and just slip off into shadow-land?

She was too far gone to feel acutely any

more. She had but one desire, to be near David, to feel his arms holding her while life lasted.

He took the coat off her tenderly, and wrung it out. He could see that her strength had greatly lessened in the last hours. What if she should die before he could climb the rope to find salvation for them? For he knew that he could never pull her up with him.

He must go alone and leave her again. What would it mean even if he did get out? He might be an hour finding help; would she be alive when he returned?

Yes, because he would first reach the car and his flask of brandy and return and throw it down to her. That would give her courage and strength.

But meanwhile she seemed faint again. He clasped her in his arms and murmured love words, and as ever this revived her, and she opened her eyes.

"David," she pleaded, "may we not lie down and rest just for a few moments? And then you can be strong and throw the rope up. . . . I am so . . . tired, darling."

The situation was very desperate, because they both were wet and shivering, and there was nothing left dry but the garments tied onto the rope. David's vest and coat tied together would make it twice as long as the blanket now made it.

He must untie that and take it to wrap Laline in. She would die of cold if she remained in her dripping crêpe-de-chine under-garments.

"Darling, I must undress you first," he whispered tenderly. "Slip off those wet things and I'll wrap you in this dry, warm blanket."

She obeyed him mechanically, and he folded the coarse coverlet round her slender form, and lifting her carried her to the corner by the biscuit tins, and laid her down.

She lay inert. Only her eyes followed David's movements, unutterable love in their hollow depths. Then the comfort of the dry woollen stuff enveloped her and her lids closed, for the unconsciousness of exhaustion had come.

He bent over her in fear.

There was not a moment to be lost. He must now make his preparations to reach the opening. The knotting of the substitutes for the blanket took no time, nor did the fixing of them to the bar of iron.

It was strange how heavy the thing felt. A thinnish bar of iron with a nut on the end of it, and it seemed to weigh a ton!

He dragged the big wooden case over almost beneath the hole in the roof, having carefully removed three cards to the other corner, keeping their faces downwards.

Then, carrying the bar, he climbed up on the box and looked upward.

The aperture seemed very far off, and if the bar did not reach it and fell back on his head, it might kill him before he could get out of the way, unless he jumped aside immediately.

Fortunately, he had been a very fine exponent of the art of throwing the javelin. It would stand him in good stead now.

He calculated the distance, and saw that his foothold was firm and that he could be sure of keeping perfect balance.

It was a bit of luck, the nut being still on the end of the bar, for he could be more sure of attaining his object and making it fall across the hole.

He gave one last look at Laline. She was either asleep or unconscious. The uncertainty seemed to give him more desperate determination. He got off the case and went over to her.

How he loved her! Every atom of her frail body, every aspect of her pure, devoted soul, which had emerged beyond the dross of earthly things.

Nothing he could ever do in afterlife, if it was going to be given to them, could be enough to show his utter worship of her.

"My darling!" he cried softly.

Then he rose and sprang on to the case once more, some fresh spurt of life and strength animating him.

He picked up the javelin, for such, indeed, the bar of iron must appear to him, and he stood poised like a Greek bronze of an athlete, and then with one mighty effort he hurled the thing up through the hole and into the space beyond.

For one agonising second he watched, and then it fell on the floor above and he pulled the rope and dragged it across the opening as he had hoped he could.

"Thank God!" he cried aloud. "Thank God!"

But the strain had been terrible, and now he half fell from the case and staggered to where Laline lay, unheeding. The rope was fast, and when he had rested a minute he must climb up it.

Rest. Yes, that is what he craved, to rest just for a few moments beside his darling.

He lay down, panting, and pulled a corner of the blanket over himself.

Then he bent over the unconscious girl. Her face was as white as death. Had her spirit fled? Was all too late, all a mockery?

In frantic anxiety he moved the blanket and put his ear to her heart. He could not be certain that he heard it beat.

And there was hope—nay, certainty—of life in front of them, for the distance was much less than the height he had climbed before, and the knots were nearer. What could he do, what could he do to keep life in her until he could reach the car?

She had given up the last bit of food to save him. What sacrifice could he make for her in return?

In a lightning-like flash an idea came to him, and without a moment's hesitation he put it into effect.

Laline's little wet chemise lay stretched out on the biscuit tins. He took it and tore it into strips; then he made a tourniquet with one bit round his left arm by the wrist, using his pocket comb for the purpose, and with another part he made a slip-knot round his arm higher, near the elbow, that he could pull right with his teeth.

Then he opened the sharp blade of his pocket-knife and cut a vein on the outside of his arm.

The blood spurted out and he let it drip into Laline's mouth.

The effect was marvellous. She opened her eyes, those grey eyes which had but lately gazed at him with the soft glance of an angel, and a wild fierceness came into them while she eagerly sucked the blood.

Then consciousness returned, and just as David had done earlier, she realised what she was doing, and with one wild shriek of horror she rolled over on her face.

Now, David has miscalculated the effect this

loss of blood would have upon him, and, just sensible enough then to pull the slip-knot tight with his teeth and stop the bleeding, he fell forward in a dead faint.

After a moment or two of mad misery Laline started up into a sitting position, the blanket falling from her, so she shivered in her nakedness, and then her eyes caught sight of a bayonet which had pinned a card to the floor.

She did not see the other ones, which were beyond the tins, behind her head. She only registered the fact that here was some kind of dagger.

She had drunk David's blood. He was dead and she would kill herself. But with some subconscious modesty, not knowing what she did, she pulled the blanket round her first, and then staggered to her feet and tottered across the floor.

The weapon was through a card. How had it got there? And the card would surely be the nine of spades, since all was death and horror round her.

She bent and pulled out the thing, which she now knew was a bayonet, and the card stuck to the point and came away with it.

She looked at it in some kind of fierce fury. And lo! the smiling face of the Queen of Hearts met her wild eyes. No sinister nine of spades, which she had expected.

Was it an omen?

Was David not dead after all? Might they still be saved?

She flung down the cold rusty steel with a gasp of revulsion, and staggered back to her love.

The faintest trickle of blood still came from his arm. With shaking fingers she pulled the slip-knot tighter, so that the bleeding stopped entirely;

then she rubbed his brow and his other hand, while she murmured tender entreaties to him to hear her.

Then she somehow got to her feet again, and gazed round frantically, and she saw the pitcher standing by the book of prayers. She went to it. They had come through water, that's why she was naked. They had been wet. But where was the water? She could not remember.

She thought and thought, and something took her to the door. Yes, there it gleamed, but far beneath. The four feet appeared to her an immense distance. She could never reach it.

Slowly, slowly, her mind worked and she looked round once more as if asking for council of some invisible presence; then her eye caught the remaining strips of her chemise, which David had torn up to make the bandage. She could tie these to the handle of the pitcher and let it down.

It took an absurdly long time to do this simple thing, but at last it was accomplished and the jug was in her hands, more than a quarter full of the dirty water.

She drank some eagerly and then took it over to David, and sprinkled it on his face, and poured it into his mouth, but he never stirred or awakened.

Ah, God! He was dead after all. There was nothing that human aid could do any more. She would lie down and die beside him.

Unless . . . yes . . . there was the book of prayers . . . and prayers could work miracles.

It was a terrible exertion to get across the floor again to where the book lay, but she succeeded in bringing it close at last, and there under the candles she opened it.

Alas, it was all in Latin!

But never mind, God would understand even if she did not. He would know she was praying for her beloved to recover, praying for herself that if it was death, their souls might go up together into Paradise and never be parted.

She saw the row of things David had taken out of the pocket of the wet coat, and she found his watch among them.

It was nearly five o'clock on Monday morning. She would read the prayers over and over until she should fall on her darling's body. And that would mean death . . . and then would come the Awakening.

And so she began, but in less than a quarter of an hour the book dropped from her nerveless fingers, and she fell forward and lay with her head on her loved one's breast while her eyes closed in merciful unconsciousness.

*   *   *

Perhaps it was the sense of her nearness which called the spirit of David to life, or perhaps the prayers had been answered, for after half-an-hour he came back to remembrance of things, and opened his black eyes, and blinked in the light of the candles.

Then he started up to a sitting position, and Laline's head slipped to his knees.

What was that? Was it a call? A call of his name? and her name?

"David—Laline . . ."

"David, are you down there?" Then a glad shout, and yes, it was old Jack's voice. Help was coming. They were going to be saved.

"Here!" David yelled with all his feeble

strength, and then he became faint and giddy once more.

*   *   *

Jack had come on down the staircase into the first-floor dug-out, and turned on his torch, while he still shouted. The roof had almost fallen in, except in one part just above the opening to the lower storey.

He went over there, and then saw the iron bar across the hole, with the arms of the coat tied to it, but the torch was so bright that he could not see the faint light coming up through the aperture.

He shouted to Fergusson to follow him with the brandy, and other restoratives which were in his bag he carried, and then he knelt down and again shouted.

"David—Laline—David, are you down there?" And to his wildly anxious ears there came a quavering voice:

"Here!"

But by this time he was descending by the rope with feverish rapidity.

What could those two poor creatures, whom he now caught sight of, have suffered?

David, with greenish olive face, and black stubbly beard, all unclothed but for his gauze nether garment, his arm smeared with blood, lay there unconscious; and Laline, close beside him, was naked except for a blanket!

Wrapped in rugs and overcoats, the rescue party arrived about eight o'clock in the morning. David was still very dazed and half-unconscious, and Laline was vague and wandering.

Mrs Greening went wild with relief and excitement, and had to be removed from the scene in hysterics. But Celestine kept her head, and put her beloved lamb to bed, and hung over her with the doctor.

Jack had been too deeply touched emotionally to show any outward sign of his feelings. But his heart was numb with anguish.

What had happened between his friend and his love in those five days underground? But this was not the moment for speculation. All he must think of was how he could help to restore them to health.

Fergusson, in his canny Scotch way, had been busy calculating.

He knew that to keep his word and be at the Embassy in time on the morrow, which was the end of the six days, would matter to his master, when once he became fully conscious, more than anything else in the world.

Therefore, it was his duty to prepare everything in readiness for their instantaneous departure as soon as Major Lamont was strong enough to travel.

If he watched over him and carried out the doctor's orders all that day, and that night, they could probably leave the next morning at ten o'clock and reach Paris in time to keep the appointment.

Fergusson was to accompany Major Lamont as far as the first place where he would disappear from the eyes of men.

He knew the importance of the mission. So all that day he nursed his master as a mother would a sick child, ministering to him with a tenderness and solicitude which no one could have guessed his taciturn nature was capable of.

"We don't want no one fussing round," he

declared, and more than once or twice kept even Jack from entering the room to ask if anything was wanted.

It would be better that none of the party knew of their flitting until after they had gone, in case they should try to prevent them from starting.

"He might give way on account of the lassie, he being so weak now," Fergusson mused, "and then he'd be fit to kill me afterwards for not getting him off, dead or alive."

So he kept his own counsel as to his plans, and got the two-seater ready.

David had a naturally splendid constitution, and he recovered with great rapidity under the wisely administered stimulants and sips of milk and chicken broth, and towards night he fell into a profound natural slumber, deep and dreamless.

Jack understood that rest was best for him, and left him alone with Fergusson.

Laline's case was more serious.

She was suffering from cold as well as exhaustion, and lay in a semi-conscious kind of torpor all day long, seemingly indifferent to everything.

But the doctors assured the distracted Jack and her Aunt and the devoted maid that she would probably be much better on the morrow, and rest and warmth and the proper sort of food was the only thing she wanted.

And so at last the morning of the sixth day came, and at nine o'clock Fergusson awakened his master. He had left him to the last possible moment.

It seemed as though his spirit came back from a long, long way, but at length he rubbed his eyes and sat up.

"I expect I'm all right now, Fergusson," he

said. "I seem to have slept forever. What day is it?"

Fergusson's face was like a mask.

"It's Tuesday, the end of your leave, sir. I've been thinking that you'd be wanting to be at the Embassy on time, sir, and so I've everything ready."

David got out of bed. So he could "take the message to Garcia" after all.

"That's fine," he answered, and his voice sounded glad. "You are a trump, Fergusson."

"Your bath is prepared, sir, in the bathroom. A mighty way off. These French hotels are pretty poor places. I'll see you safely through it, in case you were to feel faint, sir, and then I'll go and pay the bill, and have the car outside, ready to leave the minute you're ready."

And all this was carried out, but while David lay in the warm water, his whole mind was set upon what he must say to Laline. His first words to Fergusson, after their arrangements were made, were to ask about her.

Fergusson had seen Celestine at eight o'clock, bringing up more hot milk, and she had said her lady was sleeping peacefully, and that the doctor had said she was on no account to be disturbed until she awakened later.

It was obvious to David that he could not speak to her. This was terrible, but he must do his duty. He would dress as quickly as he possibly could, and while Fergusson was paying the bill, he would write to her.

Two months was not so very long to wait. He had not the least doubt that she would trust him and understand everything.

Chapter
Seven

Now, there come turns in all our lives when fate seems to tangle the threads with deliberate devilish maliciousness.

A great love cannot come into fulfilment and peace before it has passed through the heights and the depths of proof, and indeed endured the acid test. It is the little loves which go by merrily and smoothly.

Now such a turn came quickly to Laline and David, just when everything seemed fair, when they had escaped a dreadful death, and appeared to have earned the right to happiness.

It was a wonderful letter which he wrote, rapidly, to his beloved that May morning at Amiens. It told her in as few words as possible of his undying love and worship of her, and of how she must trust him, and tell no one but Jack of their wedding until he returned.

"I am on something great for our country, darling," he wrote, "and so there must be no talk or interest about me."

He explained how he must be absent for two

months, and that she must send a letter to the Grand Hotel at Rome, to await his arrival on his return journey.

"It will be wisest for you to tell Jack everything, my darling," he wrote, "and give him my real heartfelt thanks, because he's the whitest man I've ever met, and he'll protect and take care of you, no matter what pain it is to him.

"I've only been sensible enough to think this morning, and now there is no time for me to see him myself, and perhaps you would prefer to tell him in your own way, anyhow. . . ."

Then with fondest expressions of worship and love, he signed himself: "Your own loving husband, *David*."

* * *

Fergusson was still below, arranging things, so his master rang the bell for the chambermaid. He had always felt that Mrs Greening was against her niece's friendship with him, and he imagined that the maid might be antagonistic too.

But if he tipped the chambermaid well, there would be no reason for her not to deliver the note immediately on Laline's awakening. Either of the others might put it by until later.

The buxom Frenchwoman answered the bell, and received her instructions on how she was to put the letter into *Mademoiselle* Lester's own hands as soon as she awakened.

The whole hotel were, of course, highly interested in the hero and heroine of so exciting an adventure, so he had no need to explain who *Mademoiselle* Lester was.

Marie, all smiling sympathy, was not altogether inspired by David's magnificent pourboire.

She liked romance, which she scented here. *Monsieur* could count upon her; the beautiful *Mademoiselle* should have it.

And the missive was safely stowed in her apron's capacious pocket.

She was to go in at eleven with fresh hot-water bottles, she said, and would place it in the hand of *Mademoiselle* herself.

Fergusson then appeared on the scene to say that the car was at the door, all was paid, and they could start immediately.

Off they went, in the sunshine of the beautiful spring morning, and soon were whirling to Paris, the servant driving, and David trying to steady his nerves and collect his senses.

At noon a pale, gaunt, but determined young man was ushered into the American Ambassador's private sitting-room.

"Well, how splendid of you to turn up after all, Lamont," said Mr Randolph, shaking David's hand in sympathy and appreciation, "exactly on time! I never expected to see you after what I understand you've been through. A nice adventure, surely? You are looking a pretty wilted youngster. Are you certain you are fit to go on today, boy?"

There was concern as well as anxiety in his tone.

"I am quite ready, sir."

The Ambassador sighed in relief.

"I have kept everything that was possible from the press, and your name has never appeared in print at all; only the most guarded accounts of the accident were allowed to go to the editors last night. How's Miss Lester?"

David had not seen her before he left, he told His Excellency, but he believed she was progressing.

"I came straight on the moment I awakened, sir."

The Ambassador was a man of business, one who stuck always to essentials.

Major Lamont was not dead, and the very important matter, the carrying out of which he alone was quite suitable to be entrusted with, could go ahead after all, and there was no time to be lost, for the thing was too grave to afford Major Lamont too much sympathy.

Because of the strike on the Italian railways, everything was out of gear, and the express would start for Rome at one-fifteen instead of later in the day as usual.

"I have ventured to take a liberty with you, Major Lamont," Mr Randolph went on, when all the official orders had been thoroughly gone into and David was about to leave.

"I have just had a man go to the Ritz to take all your belongings to the station with my niece's luggage, Mrs Hamilton. My car's waiting below and will whirl you to the Ritz to pick up Mrs Hamilton and get you to the station in time."

David's whole mind was fixed upon the feat of registering intricate verbal instructions; he hardly took in these last words the Ambassador said, and never for one moment dreamed of the sinister turn they heralded in his fate.

"Of course, sir," he murmured absently. "I shall be delighted to do anything. My servant went straight on to the Ritz, and he will have met your man and got everything fixed."

Then they shook hands again. But as David reached the door Mr Randolph called him back, and his tone of voice was significant.

"Major Lamont, I am sure I need not reiterate that you are trusted not to communicate with

a living human being until I see you again. You
are aware of the reason for this, I know, and I
hope we are not asking a terribly hard thing of a
free young man."

His voice lightened and he smiled.

"But you were warned about this, weren't
you, before you started from Washington?"

"You have my word, sir."

All the way to the Ritz, every force of David's brain, which he knew must probably be
weakened by the hardship he had passed through,
was concentrated upon his instructions.

If he made one mistake, or forgot one point,
it might cost him his life, and, what was much
worse to him, cause his mission to fail.

He must hold himself together with an iron
hand. He still felt very weak and shaky, but he
knew this was only a temporary state of things, and
that each hour he was recovering more.

He had not had an instant in which to think
of Laline since he had reached Paris, but whenever
he was not dozing on the journey up, his mind had
never left her.

Another, less-disciplined character would have
allowed emotion to master him, and would
have made him insist upon seeing Laline, at the
risk of creating a scene, and making complica-
tions which might have retarded his departure.

But above everything David was balanced,
and made of stern stuff. His honour was engaged
in this trust which had been placed in him by the
highest powers in his country, and, having given
every tender assurance in his letter to Laline, he
knew no further perturbations.

His golden girl, who had proved herself to
have the most noble and most trusting soul, would

fully understand him, and would wait in loving faith and security for his return, and Jack would care for and protect her.

He could always count on Jack.

Meanwhile, he must not let a single thing detract from the concentration he must give to his mission.

* * *

Mrs Greening was sufficiently calm by that morning to go into her niece's room.

Celestine had never left her beloved mistress all night, untiring in her devotion since the moment Laline had been brought to Amiens, and Mrs Whitmore also had kept her head.

Laline was now sleeping peacefully, and although she was still very weak, she was certainly on the road to recovery.

Celestine put her finger to her lips when Mrs Greening appeared, and she drew her into her own room, next door.

Here, she gave an account of the night and what nourishment *Mademoiselle* had taken and how she had been.

"When I think of that Major Lamont," Mrs Greening exclaimed, "the cause of all this trouble, I wish to goodness I could wring his neck! You must not let him come near Miss Lester, Celestine, for I am through with this nonsense."

Celestine informed her that for the time being there would be no need for them to bother, because as she had gone down the stairs at ten o'clock she had chanced to see into the yard where the cars started from, through the staircase window, and there was Major Lamont and his servant, leaving, with their suitcases!

"You don't say," said Mrs Greening, relieved.

Their talking had disturbed the patient, however, and a feeble voice called:

"Celestine!"

The two women rushed back into the room to find that Laline was fully awake and looking better.

Mrs Greening fussed as much as she dared, for Celestine's eye was sternly upon her. Then she was wise enough to leave as soon as she could, on the plea of meeting the doctor.

The moment Laline was alone with her maid she whispered:

"Celli ... how is Major Lamont? ... And when can he come to see me?"

"Monsieur le Major has departed for Paris, *Mademoiselle.* I see him go at ten o'clock."

Laline's face blanched.

"He's ... gone to ... Paris."

"It would seem so." Celestine shrugged her shoulders; she now knew that she was giving her lamb great pain, and she hated having to do so.

"But doubtless *le Major* had duties and will communicate with *Mademoiselle* presently."

"He's left no letter for me, then?"

Laline's still-languid voice sharpened with anxiety and she started up in bed.

"Are you sure, Celestine *chère?* Go down to the concierge at once and ask ... and will you also ask Captain Lumley?"

But Celestine was full of fear when she saw her little mistress's face. She must be soothed and quieted before she could leave her.

This, however, only enraged Laline.

"Go ... go at once ... I cannot bear it!" she cried brokenly.

Celestine went, but returned in a few min-

utes with the news that Captain Lumley was still
in bed, sleeping, after having been up all night,
and Major Lamont had left at ten with Fergusson,
his servant, who had given no information as to
their destination.

The servant had paid the bill, and *le Monsieur*
had come rapidly through the hall and got into
the car. That is all the concierge knew about it!

Laline trembled as she lay in bed. What
could this mean? She was too weak to reason.

"Ask the chambermaid and the waiter . . .
perhaps he left some note with them."

Celestine departed again on this mission, but
returned, no one had received any message. She
did not know that it was a different chambermaid
on the floor where David had slept, who was now
on duty.

Laline could not believe her ears, and in her
weak state she burst into a passion of tears.

"Oh! You are all wrong . . . you are all deceiving me. Auntie hates Major Lamont . . . and
you are a cruel, wicked woman, Celli. . . ."

The devoted maid was now beside herself
with sorrow and commiseration. She felt that she
would tell any lie to quiet her lamb—but what,
what, could she say?

The Major had gone, and that seemed the end
of it.

The doctor was now coming in to the next
room, she heard him.

"I will go once more," she assured Laline,
"and question again, but my *Mademoiselle chérie*
must quiet herself."

Laline sobbed less violently, and Celestine escaped into the adjoining apartment. There she
confided in the doctor, Mrs Greening fortunately
being absent.

Her *Mademoiselle* had received disquieting news and was in a state of great agitation. Might not a good *piqûre* be a fine thing to quiet the nerves until she was stronger?

Monsieur le docteur would know.

The doctor agreed with Celestine as soon as he saw his patient's poor little face. Laline held herself as well as she could while he was talking to her, but her eyes stared in an agonised way.

They kept her dozing all that day and night, and when Wednesday came she awoke, stronger in health, but with the awful sense of calamity crushing upon her.

Now, all this trouble came about because fate had used as an instrument the unmended hole in the apron pocket of a chambermaid in a provincial French hotel.

Marie, the woman in question, was not at all a bad creature, and she had had every intention of delivering the letter from so generous a gentleman to so beautiful a lady.

But what will you? She had meant to mend the hole yesterday but had forgotten, and the wretched thing had grown larger and larger, so that without her being aware of it, the letter at last slipped through the hole and onto the floor.

It fell among the torn-up papers of a commercial traveller in one of the other rooms which she was doing, and was duly carried away and burnt with the rest of the debris, by Antoine, *le valet de chambre,* and so that was that!

When the time came for her to go to Miss Lester's room to replenish the hot-water bottles, she was just about to knock at the door, and felt for the envelope, and there she perceived the hole, and her pocket's emptiness.

Aghast, for a moment she paused, undecided as to what to do; then she went directly back to the room she had come from, but found that Antoine had already departed with the rubbish.

Then, in doubt, she dived into her dress pocket for her purse, and gave a great sigh of relief—*Monsieur*'s fifty-franc note was safe fortunately, so the gravest part of her anxiety was quieted.

And again, what will you? Accidents will happen, and after all, the letters of young gentlemen to young ladies were never serious affairs, and these two would doubtless meet in Paris in a day or so, and *Mon Dieu!* the thing was gone, and that was the end of it. But her pourboire was not lost.

Better to say nothing and pretend to know nothing, since her intentions had been good, and just ill luck had stepped in and frustrated them.

Her shoulders shrugged eloquently, and presently, the bottles filled, she went on with her work happily, and later ate an excellent *déjeuner*.

Jack Lumley came down at lunch-time, refreshed from his short rest, and Celestine told him that her mistress was sleeping.

Laline was in no state to think clearly for another twenty-four hours, and it was late Wednesday afternoon when she awoke to full consciousness.

She was alone in the room for the moment. At first her eyes took in the buff-coloured, striped paper, the heavy *garniture de cheminée*, and the stiff furniture.

The window was wide open and the softly scented spring air came in to her.

Why did she feel this frightful sense of depression? And where was she?

Yes, she knew that she was in the hotel at

Amiens, and that she and David had been saved, but had not David gone? She must think deeply. Yes, that was it, David had left her.

When this thought came, she started up in bed and called shrilly: "Celestine!" but it was Mrs Whitmore who entered the room, and not her faithful Nannie.

"Oh, Laline! We're so glad you are awake and all right, dear. I'm just sitting here while Celestine rests a little bit. Why, you don't look too fine, child—do you want some milk or anything?"

Laline wanted only one thing, news of David, and that, she feared, Mrs Whitmore could not give her, but she was a proud girl and not accustomed to letting her secrets out. So, even in her feeble state, she had sense enough to manoeuvre.

"How's everybody?" she asked as lightly as she could. "You all must have been crazy with anxiety about us."

"Indeed we were, and we are longing to hear just what happened."

"Major Lamont can tell you better than I. . . ."

"But he's gone—he went yesterday morning while you were still unconscious, dear; very strange of him, I do think."

Laline fired up. No one should speak slightingly of her David.

"He had business in Paris, of course . . . and please, I don't want to talk of that horrible time for ages and ages. You can't think what it is to be starved to death and in darkness."

She shivered.

"We just went into the dug-out for fun to see the place where Jack and Major Lamont fought. An old priest showed us the way, but he was killed in the explosion."

She shut her eyes for a moment.

"I think I'll try and sleep again now, Mrs Whitmore. Please don't wait, I am all right. Just send Celestine to me when she wakes up."

As soon as she was alone in the room again, a fearful restlessness overcame her. What possibly could be the meaning of things? David had always been mysterious about his movements, she remembered.

What *was* his business? He had said once that he had to do what he must sometimes, but was hoping someday to do what he could. Had he received some order?

But even so, to leave her without a word! Her David . . . her very own husband!

She was trembling all over now.

She did not doubt him. She loved him utterly, but there surely must be some explanation. Perhaps he had left it with Jack, and Celestine did not know about it. She would send for Jack the very moment she could.

How was she to bear this uncertainty? It was much worse a pain than any she had gone through in the dug-out.

But above everything she must not mistrust David. She felt her wedding ring. Where was her great sapphire, which her father had given her? She did not care very much. How could a ring matter now? How could anything matter?

David was the beginning and ending of her horizon.

Would Celestine never come? Must she lie there inert and helpless?

They would leave immediately for the Ritz; there, of course, there would be a letter for her, or probably David himself. And so her thoughts wandered, in incessant speculations.

He had hated all the fuss made by her Aunt and the Whitmores, that was probably it, and had gone off thinking she would recover quickly and, of course, return to Paris.

Perhaps he was making all the arrangements with the Ambassador for their civil wedding. Things were so strange, and she must not let evil possibilities come into her mind, but only good ones.

She would not tell her Aunt or Jack anything about her marriage to David; they would tell it together when she was with him in Paris.

There her heart beat, at the thought of being with him in Paris! Oh! how glorious.

She must not let a single thing trouble her now, since it was obvious to anyone who had any horse sense that no man who had been her lover and husband for five days, and with whom she had faced the possibility of a horrible death, could go off directly they were saved, with the deliberate intention of deserting her!

And so some comfort came, at length, and she lay still.

Then her thoughts were back to the beginning of their married hours, and she thrilled at her remembrances.

"I would so much like to see Captain Lumley," Laline said, when Mrs Whitmore came back to see her. "Would you please ask him to come up . . . if he is in the hotel? I am quite all right now."

"Surely, dear." And with a good deal more talking, Mrs Whitmore left her at length, and presently Jack came to her.

"Laline, my darling!" he cried brokenly. "Oh, how thankful I am that you are better!"

"I'm all right, Jack," she said cheerily, her

statement in contrast to her lily-white face and blue-shadowed eyes.

He came over close to the bed and sat down beside her.

"Laline, you can never know the frightful pain these days have been; I just can't talk about it, but you can guess." And he kissed her nearly transparent hand.

"Yes, dear Jack, you are so good and kind. Did . . . Major Lamont leave any message with you before he went?"

"No, and wasn't it odd of him? It is the strangest thing I've ever known; for old David to hop off like that, I suppose he had some important appointment."

Laline could feel that sensation as of an icy hand pressing her heart, that feeling of sick emptiness which is so hard to endure. She longed to tell everything to this kind friend, but she could not.

Where could she begin? Where break off? It would all pain him horribly, and it might be better to wait until they reached Paris, and David was with them again . . . with them again. . . . But would he be with them again?

And once more the agonising feeling of mystery, uncertainty, and misery came over her.

Jack was much too sympathetic a person to allude to the horror of the five days in the dug-out.

He contented himself by telling her, in as commonplace a string of sentences as he could, of how they at last had found them, and about the rescue, as Laline had been unconscious until they had reached the car.

It had taken longer to bring David round.

"His arm was cut, and he had a tourniquet on it, and a bandage above to stop the bleeding.

We did wonder how that had happened. You were knocked out, and I expect did not know anything about it, dear little girl. The poor old boy must have lost a lot of blood."

Laline shut her eyes for a moment. She was controlling herself, with difficulty, and trying, trying to remember clearly.

David was holding his arm over her mouth, she could reconstruct that picture, and now she realised that he must have made preparations for the bleeding beforehand, since the tourniquet and the slip-knot were already on his arm.

Was it . . . could it be . . . that he had cut a vein deliberately, to pour the blood into her mouth in an effort to save her if she was fainting?

Yes, that must have been it! Dear, noble David. Her love . . . her darling . . . her husband! *But where was he?*

Jack saw that something had moved her exceedingly, for she had lain back, trembling, with tears coming from her quivering, closed eyelids.

"We won't speak about anything to do with the frightful time, dearest child," he said, tender solicitude in his tone. "We'll only talk of joining old David quickly in Paris."

Laline opened her eyes, and gratitude was in their depths.

Then Jack soothed her, and suggested that he should come and sit with her while she had her dinner, which consisted of some chicken and green peas and champagne, and other good things!

Laline was glad to have him. Anything was better than being alone with her thoughts, and nothing could possibly be done until they reached Paris the next morning.

Then the doctor arrived, and felt her agitated

pulse, and decided that for this one more night a sleeping draught would not hurt her.

Jack knew she was frightfully anxious to know what had made David go so suddenly, and, as he could not help her, he did his utmost to keep her mind engaged with other things.

They spoke of Channings Priory. How he hoped she would like it! It was a dear old place, with cloisters going to the Chapel, and it would be looking its best now with all the fresh greenery.

Laline tried to answer interestedly, tried to talk, tried to control herself. But all the time some inward voice was saying:

"Where are you? David, come back to me! Oh, where can you be?"

But presently the old doctor returned and gave her the draught, and so at last she slept soundly, and in the morning, although the poor child could hardly stand on her feet, the party went back by train to Paris, and arrived at the Ritz Hotel about lunch-time.

It was with perfectly feverish anxiety that Laline asked for her mail when they arrived at the Ritz Hotel.

It was a large bunch of envelopes, but all from America, except one from her friend Molly, who had married the English Marquis.

Molly was enchanted to hear that Laline had arrived in Europe, and she had sent a cordial invitation for Laline to stay with her in London.

All this once would have been a delight, but now Laline could hardly take in the sense of the words, so great had been the blow of finding no word from David.

She would ask the concierge; perhaps there was some message for her at his desk, rather than with the mail clerk. Messages and letters sometimes did go wrong in hotels.

There were some cards and notes which had already gone up to the sitting-room, she was informed, and then it seemed as if no lift ever went so slowly!

But at last she was there in the sunny room, which looked upon the garden.

Mrs Greening was fussing all the time, but Laline paid no attention to her. Her fingers trembled so that she could not hold the American letters which she carried, and Jack took them from her hands.

Then she hastily scanned the few cards, and two notes, which lay on the table. None was from David. She felt very faint, and sank into an armchair.

"Why, my dear, you'll just pass out if you don't take care of yourself!" her Aunt exclaimed. "Go lie down this minute."

Jack supported her into the bed-room, and Celestine laid her on the sofa, and motioned them all to leave her mistress alone with her. Laline's eyes had told her much.

When the door was closed, the poor girl raised herself up and clung to the maid's arm.

"Celli, I'm going crazy. I must know where Major Lamont is. You must go down as if on your own, and question the concierge if he came here, and if so, where is he?"

Celestine went to the telephone and asked if Major Lamont was in the hotel.

Laline watched her face anxiously. She could see that nothing she wished to know was being told.

"Go down and find out everything. I can't bear it any longer!"

Celestine covered her mistress with the eiderdown, for she was shivering so.

"Please go!"

Her Aunt joined her, and she was nearly at breaking point. How could she go on bearing the chatter of her Aunt!

"I am sure Jack's waiting for his lunch, dear. Do go, I'm all right," she pleaded, "and I want to be quiet and eat this lovely omelette."

Mrs Greening assured her that she was in no hurry, and in desperation Laline cried out:

"Well, I'm just so nervous I can't eat with anyone here!"

This had its effect, and when her Aunt had gone, Celestine came up close to her.

She had questioned everyone, she told her mistress, pretending it was Fergusson she particularly wanted to hear news of, and she had gathered that *Monsieur le Major*—and here she paused awkwardly, for it was so terrible to her to be the bringer of such bad news.

"Go on, for mercy's sake, Nannie."

"*Eh bien!* Well, *Monsieur le Major* arrived on Tuesday about half-an-hour after his servant, who packed, and with the lady's maid started for the Gare de Lyon. . . ."

"What lady's maid?" Laline's voice was icy, and her face had grown deadly white, while her grey eyes flashed fiercely.

"Ze lady with whom *Monsieur le Major* went to Rome."

"Celli, for God's sake, speak out . . . tell me everything!"

So the maid began again in detail. How Fergusson had arrived and another servant, and with Mrs Hamilton's maid . . .

"Mrs Hamilton!" Laline hissed, interrupting.

Celestine went on to say that then that lady had waited in the hall most impatiently, asking constantly if Major Lamont had arrived, for they would be late, and finally he drove up in a car, rushed in to meet her, and they both went off in the same car to the Gare de Lyon.

"They were en route to Rome, *Mademoiselle*, because the *chasseur* who helped to take the luggage from the Ritz saw them together in the carriage as the train left the station."

But Laline heard no more for a few moments, as she had fainted.

When she came to herself she was still alone with Celestine, who with an agonised face knelt on the floor beside her.

The poor distracted child gazed at her maid pitifully.

"Celli ... Celli ... let me die. I can't bear it."

"My lamb ... my dove ..."

"You are quite, quite certain that ... there can't be any mistake? Oh, he could never have done such a thing! No one could be so cruel."

Celestine could only shake her head sadly. These people below had no motive to make mischief. The facts were just as she had said.

"Then there is no truth on earth or in Heaven."

Laline's voice was terrible, and no one would have recognised the haggard face, with drawn mouth and stony eyes, as her sweet, soft one.

What agony she suffered in the next hour no one could gauge. She sobbed and cried, and then lay still, but trembling. She got up from the sofa and went to the window.

Should she throw herself out and have done with the hideous anguish?

Celestine filled a tumbler of champagne

from the pint which the Amiens doctor had ordered Miss Lester to take at her meals, until she should be quite recovered, and she went over and made her drink it.

Then she sat by her and stroked her hair, and coaxed her to eat some tender chicken, and finally she appealed to her pride.

Mrs Greening and Captain Lumley would be coming up in a minute, and they surely must not see *Mademoiselle* like this!

Laline straightened herself.

"Don't let them come in . . . say I am asleep!" And she flung herself down on the bed.

Celestine locked the door.

* * *

Jack was allowed to have lunch with Laline in the sitting-room, and nothing could exceed his kindness, and his dear sympathy seemed to lap her round with warmth and comfort.

She had fought with herself in the dawn when she awoke. Even with all these proofs of David's defection, ought she to condemn him until she could see him face to face?

No, she ought not. He would not have opened a vein in his arm to save her life if he were such a false deceiver. There still must be some explanation, and she would calm herself and say her prayers, those prayers she had so often repeated in the dug-out.

Ah, how happy she had been there! And how much better if they had just died together and never come back to this cruel outside world, where all was false and devilish.

After she heard of the invitation to the Embassy from her Aunt in the morning, she cheered up a little, but underneath there was still this awful sinking; however, hope is a strange thing, and even this faint hope that she might have news of David gave her courage.

She went down to luncheon, a pale-lily girl, immensely interesting.

Jack was extremely worried in his mind. He knew Laline so very well. He guessed that something terrible was troubling her.

Had she quarrelled with David in some final way, that he had gone off like this? Or had David fallen violently in love with her, and, not being able to make her love him, had thought flight the wisest course?

Laline was like a white orchid in a pure white dress that night at the Embassy. She had never looked more lovely or been more attractive.

Her face now had character stamped upon it. Her beautiful eyes were no longer meaningless, but contained some story.

She had no chance of speaking to the Ambassador until after dinner, when the dance was going on, and then with the art which is truly female she turned the conversation in the way she wanted it to go, when he came up to talk to her.

She made herself speak of the accident so as to get in David's name.

Major Lamont had been so wonderful! And by the way, did His Excellency happen to know the Major's address in Rome? She wanted to write and thank him, as he had had to go off from Amiens before she was awake.

The Ambassador looked at her keenly. Had David betrayed a trust? But she gave herself away.

"We heard at the Ritz that he had left for Rome, and as your niece, Mrs Hamilton, must have gone by the same train, I wondered if you would know where to find him."

Mr Randolph's clever eyes were as innocent as a child.

He had no knowledge whatever of Major Lamont, and his manner gave the impression that he was greatly surprised to hear that he had gone to Rome with his niece!

Surprised, and not altogether pleased!

Laline was no fool, but she was unaccustomed to clever diplomats, and had never had to cross swords with one before.

"He did not know she meant to meet David," Laline thought. "They must have arranged it all at that Ball, and so he had only just time to rush off to keep the appointment."

It seemed as though her knees were giving way under her, and she sank into a chair nearby.

"I'm so sorry to still be so feeble," she said with a nervous laugh. "I suppose it takes some little while to quite recover from almost starvation!"

Then she called all her pride to her rescue. She, Laline Lester. Alas! she could no longer think of herself as "Lamont," and she *would not* let the world know that a man had betrayed and made a fool of her. She would come up to the scratch even if it killed her.

So she forced herself to be gay, and go off and dance, though she could hardly stand, and presently a brilliant pink flash came into her rosy white cheeks, and Jack thought he had never seen her look so beautiful.

But when she was alone again at the Ritz, all pretence fell from her and she paced her room in agony.

There could be no doubt now. The going off had been an arranged thing, and must have been all settled before they ever went to Amiens.

As soon as David became conscious he remembered it, and felt the easiest way was to go right off without making any excuse, to avoid her reproaches.

He knew, as she did, that there was no proof of their wedding—the priest was dead and there had not even been a ring.

Here her trembling little hands felt her own diamond hoop, which was still on her left ring finger, and with a gesture of passionate resentment she began to draw it off.

But something stopped her. No . . . not yet . . . not yet.

How could a man be such a false brute? David had teased her and made her jealous about Mrs Hamilton, she remembered now, one time when she was watching him digging.

Could it have been that he was feeling awkward, remembering about this appointment? Had his whole love for her been false . . . and were his kisses Judas's kisses?

No . . . no! Impossible. Whatever hold Mrs Hamilton had over her beloved—one evidently strong enough to make him betray every trust and break Laline's heart—while she and David had been together below the earth he had passionately loved her.

She would wait yet a week . . . two weeks . . . before she removed the ring.

And never should a word about their relations to each other pass her lips. It was merciful that she had not given this secret away to her Aunt or to Jack, or even to Celestine, on her first awakening!

And at last she went to bed, utterly worn out, and slept heavily.

And so the days passed in alternate anguish and hope and fear, until they left for England in the second week of June.

Chapter
Eight

They motored from Dover to Channings Priory, which was about a twenty-mile drive through the most divine green country; which seemed to Laline's eyes as a cultivated garden, with its velvety small fields and flowering hedges.

There was a stillness in the air, and great peace, and her troubled heart experienced a sense of relief, although she knew not why.

Laline sat by the latticed window at Channings, when she was supposed to be resting before dinner, and a sense of stupefaction came over her.

It was all too incredible, but she was not the kind of character to chase after any man.

If David was so base as to have deserted her for another woman, he would be base enough to deny that there had ever been any ceremony of marriage between them.

Her Aunt was not of a nature which would make it wise to confide in her, and if the romance of her life was over, better that it should be her own secret.

She was an utterly changed Laline from the

beautiful, self-confident, spoilt heiress of Washington days. She was very pale, and much thinner, and her eyes seemed never to have lost those blue hunger shadows.

Mrs Greening placed everything to the account of the five days underground, and Jack's devotion never flagged. He said nothing to agitate Laline about his own desires towards her. He just waited and worshipped.

"Jack, isn't life a queer thing," she said to him. "I am just beginning to understand it means that we can't trust anyone, not even ourselves."

"Don't say that, Laline, you can always trust me."

"Yes, I know."

She sighed.

"Will you do something for me? Use every means you know of to find out for me where Major Lamont is. We have heard nothing of him since the 22nd of May. He's got my sapphire ring. It came off in the dug-out when my hand got thin ... and I want it back," she added nervously.

"I have done so, dear. I've asked everyone who knows him, that I know—even a chap in the Embassy in Rome. No news of him anywhere."

"He had a friend there ... a Mrs Hamilton ... perhaps we could hear through her?" Laline whispered anxiously.

Jack had obtained the same information that Celestine had, and knew of David's departure from the Ritz with the young widow.

He had asked about her in his letter to his friend in Rome, and the reply, he feared, would further hurt Laline, which was why the subject had been dropped between them now for ten days, and he had not mentioned it to her.

"You know something, Jack?"

"Well—er—my friend said Mrs Hamilton and her sister, Princess Pinoli, had gone yachting, and there were two young Americans on board. So I suppose one is David. They went on a cruise to the Greek Islands."

Rage filled Laline now. Here she was, suffering, in anguish, and he ... her husband ... was amusing himself "among the Greek Islands"!

Mrs Greening rushed Laline up to London after a week at Channings Priory, where her friend Molly greeted her with effusiveness, and introduced her to many new acquaintances, but nothing registered in Laline's brain, and by the end of June a hideous terror had begun to haunt her dreams.

They had been in England for a fortnight and everything which could make life fair for her had been showered upon her.

"She appears wilted that way because of the dreadful starvation picnic the poor darling has been through," Mrs Greening told Molly, whom she could see was disappointed about her old school friend's appearance.

"It's affected her mind. She looks to me as though she's seen a ghost," Lady Molly Fordebrooke averred, unconvinced. "You should consult Sir James Hunter."

Laline felt that everyone was anxious about her, but when Mrs Greening suggested that this specialist should be called in, she scoffed at the idea, laughed, and put on a fresh spurt of gaiety, but insisted upon returning to Paris.

Celestine had been sent on a long-promised holiday to see her French relations, when her mistress went to England. The faithful maid had been very loth to leave her lamb, but Laline had been firm about it.

She wanted to be alone, with no one who knew her anguish near to her. Now, however, Celestine would be waiting for her at the Ritz, and this thought brought a little comfort.

It was a very hot night that first evening when they arrived, attended by Jack, as usual, and everyone was dining in the garden.

Their table was just outside the restaurant, and they had intended to go on to the theatre and so were dining early, when it was still quite light.

Everyone was gay, and the whole scene was animated as usual; the Grand Prix was just over, but many strangers were lingering on.

Suddenly, by the entrance, farther along in the garden, a tall man could be seen standing with his back to them.

Laline had been acting her part to the best of her ability; she was so bright that she had almost deceived Celestine when she dressed her. Almost, not quite.

And now she had said something with a laugh, which, however, broke into a shuddering gasp when she caught sight of the tall, black-haired figure.

"David," she whispered, with whitening lips.

Jack glanced round.

"By Jove, yes! I do believe it's the old fox!" he exclaimed excitedly, and got up from his chair to go to him.

Then the man turned round, and they saw that it was a stranger.

The shock was too much for Laline. She could control herself no longer. She started from her seat, holding her hand to her heart, and rapidly entered the open doors into the corridor, and rushed wildly up the staircase by the restaurant entrance.

Jack and Mrs Greening looked at each other, at a loss as to what to do, and then they left the table and followed the fugitive up to the sitting-room.

But, when they reached it, they found that the door into Laline's room, beyond, was locked, and they could hear Celestine soothing her.

"I believe we had better leave her alone," Jack said. "The sight of that man has evidently brought all the horror of the dug-out back to her, poor darling child."

"Celestine knows how to manage her, and you are surely right, Jack. I'll come back presently, but we had best return to our dinner."

So they went down again, but both were too preoccupied to keep up more than a pretence at a conversation.

That her niece evidently was still interested in this hateful, unimportant, home-grown Major, Mrs Greening was now convinced! Where had her pride gone since he had run away from her the moment he could after being rescued?

He must have been showing to her down there underground the same indifference that he had shown on the ship! She made up her mind that she would have a serious talk with her niece about the whole matter presently, and get at the truth of things.

This sort of scene must never be repeated. She was angry as well as disturbed. For she knew that Laline was a difficult subject to handle, and that she would be very unlikely to be influenced by her Aunt in any way.

Jack was full of pain and foreboding. He had been very uneasy ever since the rescue, but had bravely put the subject from his mind, and concentrated only upon devising how he could best soothe and divert Laline.

He too felt that some kind of explanation might be the best thing to have now.

And upstairs, in the rose-and-white bed-room, Laline was lying with her head buried in Celestine's ample breast, sobbing.

Then she lay back on the pillow with closed eyes for a second, and then she opened them and looked and looked at the maid, and there was something significant in the agony which showed in their depths, which almost caused Celestine's heart to stop beating.

"It surely ... cannot be ... ?" she whispered breathlessly. "Oh, *quelle horreur!* Oh, is *Mademoiselle* sure? Oh, *ma chérie, ma chérie!*"

Then she held the trembling girl to her passionately, and they talked rapidly for some time, and at last she said:

"The brute, the murderer, the assassin! Now we must think, we must think!"

Soon her clever French brain whispered ideas of consolation to her mistress, and finally she put her to bed and administered a sleeping draught, and in an hour Laline was asleep.

Then Celestine folded her clothes, while she pondered deeply, and made short exclamations in her own language, with incipient shrugs of her shoulders.

"Five days alone! *Mon Dieu! Que voulez-vous?* Both, so young, so handsome."

There were many alternatives, she decided, but to marry Captain Lumley at once would be the most suitable and convenient one.

Only Laline's welfare concerned her; Jack, or even a saint come to earth, would have been considered only as a means for her to use for her end.

Neither's feelings in the matter would have weighed at all with Celestine!

She did not go to bed herself, but lay beside Laline all that night on the sofa, and would not let Mrs Greening, who came up later, disturb them.

Mademoiselle was sleeping quietly and would be perfectly well on the morrow, she said. No, no doctor was necessary.

She had made up her mind. She would wait one week, and then she would act. Meanwhile, her *adorée* must be made to realise Captain Lumley's goodness and the value of his protection.

Laline had told her everything. With the priest dead, and no wedding ring, and the bridegroom absconded, who was to prove that a marriage had taken place? No one.

And even if *Monsieur le Major* could be found and forced to come back, it would obviously be against his will, since he had gone off with another lady, and think then what misery and humiliation that would be to her lamb!

And if he refused—the scandal, the unpleasantness! And by that the door closed to the other, and good, plan.

No. There was but one way out of all difficulties, and that was a speedy marriage with *le Capitaine*.

After this decision, Celestine slept. She was a practical person.

Once more Laline's waking was a nightmare. She felt too ill to get up, she said, but Celestine coaxed her to let her make her beautiful, and to allow Captain Lumley to come see her in the sitting-room.

She knew Mrs Greening intended to go to Fontainbleau with friends for the day. She felt it wiser not to disclose her plan to her lamb yet. Let her appreciate the lovely roses which Jack had just sent up to her, and be with him alone first.

So when the Aunt had safely departed at about twelve, Jack was telephoned for, and came up, to find a golden-haired, lily-white girl lying wrapped in a snowy crêpe negligé, and covered by an ermine rug, with his roses in a great vase beside her.

Celestine had attended to every detail, to make a beautiful picture, Laline herself being numb and indifferent. All desire for life was over for her, and nothing more mattered.

For if all her faithful Celli had whispered to her should prove unavailing, she meant to end things in her own way and slip into shadow-land.

And what would this knowledge, which was so cruel now, have meant to her and to David? If only . . .

She remembered that during one of their tender whisperings they had spoken of such hopes. Oh . . . the cruel, cruel agony of everything!

Jack's kind, quiet face paled when he entered the room and looked at her; there was a pathetic hopelessness about her expression, even though she smiled faintly, as he took and kissed her hand. She thanked him softly for the flowers.

"You are so kind and dear, Jack," she whispered.

Then the contrast of his love and David's brutal desertion made the tears well up in her eyes.

Jack was greatly moved.

"Baby, darling baby, what is it? Oh, if you would only let me love and take care of you always," he pleaded. "Darling, once more, will you not marry me, and let me try to comfort you and make you happy again?"

The tears were now trickling slowly down Laline's white cheeks. She buried her face in her hands.

"Jack, there is something ... I ... cannot ..."

Love seems to intensify intuition, and as Jack gazed at her, in a flash he *knew*.

For a moment he started to his feet, and then sat down again, and bent and kissed her hair. His voice was hoarse as he said:

"Laline—oh, my darling little love!—I understand everything now. . . ."

He bent closer and spoke into her ear.

"I love you more than anything on earth, and I've always said that love means devotion. Now's the time I can show it. Laline, say you will marry me immediately!"

She was utterly overcome at his goodness. What did it mean? Did he understand really? Or was it only because he thought her so unhappy about David's going?

She dropped her hands and gazed at him with mournful, despairing eyes, and she saw that his distinguished, gentle face was working with controlled emotion, and that his blue eyes were full of tears, but there was comprehension in them.

"Jack ... ?"

"I tell you, I understand," he said quickly. "David ..." And then he broke off and took both her hands and drew her to him.

"You need not tell me anything. I know. Just marry me at once, and I'll make you forget everything."

"Oh, Jack ... you glorious friend!" she

cried, brokenly. "If it's really true that you_under-
stand, and you want me still to be your wife . . .
because . . . even so . . . that would make you
happy . . . I, I . . ."

But she could not finish the sentence.

"You will marry me, darling?"

She made a faint gesture of assent, then fell
into passionate weeping. Her mind was torn with
the question of whether she should tell Jack about
the priest and the wedding.

He was kissing her little left hand now, with
only gladness in his spirit.

What did he care for anything more since
he would have her always to protect and worship?

"Jack . . . leave me . . . now, dear. I want to
think out something. . . ."

He rose, always obedient to her wishes.

"I will go as long as it is nothing which can
cause you to change your mind. Remember, darling, I never want to hear a single thing about
that awful time. I want to obliterate it entirely
from both our memories.

"David shall be a dead memory between us,
and your child shall be my child. All I ask is that
you don't tell me a thing. You are all that matters
to me. What has passed does not concern us."

"I promise, Jack," she said faintly.

He kissed her hair again and went from the
room. And when he had gone, some strange
peace fell upon Laline. Here was strength and
love indeed, and, above all, understanding.

David had broken his sacred vow and deserted and betrayed her; the priest and the ceremony meant nothing to him. No law could prove
that there ever had been a marriage.

Jack had come to her rescue, would give

her back honour and protection, and she could make him happy. She would give her life in gratitude.

No, she would not tell him anything further, for the die was cast; with a firm movement she moved her little diamond hoop ring back to her right hand again.

Celestine came in just then and Laline turned and looked at her.

"I am going to marry Captain Lumley, Celli," she said quietly; "quite soon ... perhaps in a fortnight. ..."

Celestine almost cried in her relief and satisfaction.

"He knows everything," Laline went on. "I am not deceiving him, and I will try to make up to him for his goodness."

"Quel gentilhomme!" was all Celestine could blurt out; *"Quel gentilhomme!"*

*   *   *

At that moment, far away to the southeast, David was sitting, in a waiting attitude, by a crag looking over a blue sea. His black eyes gleamed from under a Turkish fez, and he stroked his short black beard.

The mission was nearly finished, and it had been very successful. He had had some near shaves, and some moments of great danger and excitement, but some luck always protected him.

He would be able to get back to Paris about the 22nd of July, if all went well this time; it would be exactly two months since he had quitted it.

How passionately and tenderly he had thought of Laline in all these weeks! His darling —where was she, what was she doing? Could it be possible that ... ? Oh! How glorious!

Jack, of course, would be taking the greatest care of her. He could trust old Jack.

What would her first love letter to him be like, which he would find in Rome? How he longed for it!

He would be free now to dispose of his time as he pleased. His service would be over.

They would have to be married again, civilly, and then where would she want him to take her? Somewhere in the country in England, perhaps. They would motor, and he would show her all sorts of old places that he knew about.

How would she be looking? Perfectly beautiful, of course, and she would have got quite over the effects of hunger by now, just as he had done. He had never felt better in his life.

What was that noise? A stealthy movement beyond the crag behind him. He got into a defensive position and took out his revolver. Two villainous-looking Greeks peered over the top, then they came at him, their knives brandished.

Flash—flash! One fell, tripping over the crag and falling into the sea far below, and the other closed with him, pinning his arms.

They struggled and struggled, the Greek trying to push his adversary to the edge of the precipice. He was a powerful man, a giant, almost, but just when he seemed to be succeeding, David got his arm free and fired his revolver straight at the brute's head.

Then he bent over the dead body, on his face a look of disgust mingled with satisfaction, and with care he searched the inner pockets of the jacket the bandit wore, and discovered a thin leather case.

So this was the culmination of all his toil. He had secured the evidence.

Now he would but have to get back to civilisation with his life, and then for Paris, and love!

And later that day, when Laline had received the congratulations of her Aunt and of the Whitmores, and was out in the Bois du Boulogne, driving in a peaceful green *allée* with her devoted fiancé, David, her husband and lover, was fleeing before a crowd of horsemen—fleeing for his life! —over uneven ground of rough grass and crags and pines.

But Laline's eyes, full of love and trust and tenderness, seemed to call him forward into safety, and he rode like the wind.

*   *   *

Jack had made it appear to Mrs Greening that he must have an immediate wedding. Why should they wait? Had he not been asking Laline to marry him for more than half a year? And many of their friends had looked upon the engagement as an imminent certainty.

There, with all the shops in Paris to choose from, a trousseau was quite possible to get in a fortnight, or in three weeks; and could they not be married about the twentieth of July in the old Chapel at Channings Priory?

Mrs Greening was delighted at this suggestion. The old place would make a wonderful background for a wedding. It would all be so chic, and make such interesting reading for all their friends back home.

They must have a real English wedding too, with the train of bridesmaids, and little pages, and she would delight to entertain as large a party as the house would hold!

Laline and Jack would have preferred to have everything as quiet as possible, but Mrs

Greening was determined to have her way. And the sooner the ceremony could take place, the better she would be pleased, as in her secret heart she feared that Laline might change her mind!

The warm days of July went by very rapidly.

Laline had asked Jack to go back to England and arrange all his affairs, so as to be quite ready to take her away after the wedding, to some quiet place in Switzerland, where they would spend the rest of the summer and the autumn.

She felt that she would want to be far from scenes which could remind her of anything she had ever known before.

She resolutely shut her eyes now to the future, which she vaguely felt must eventually be happy, since Jack was so good and kind and so devoted to her, and she sternly banished thoughts of the past whenever they presented themselves.

She was in all ways growing into a stronger character. David's influence was insidious; unconsciously, she was putting into practice that self-restraint and discipline which he had often talked to her about in their long hours, and which she knew was what he thought essential to the making of a personality which he could respect.

Celestine was the only creature now who saw any signs of her grieving.

"She is but twenty-two years, and *le Capitaine* is so considerate, sorrow will pass."

The trousseau was chosen, and the days were full of feverish trying on of clothes and hats, and the evenings passed in feasting with American friends, of whom shoals appeared to be in Paris.

So that when bed-time came each night, Laline was too tired to think, and fell into dreamless slumber. But, underneath, her subconscious mind was uneasy, haunted always by a doubt.

Could there possibly be any mistake? Could it possibly be that she was being unjust to David?

But nothing happened to influence her one way or another about this, and the sixteenth of the month came, and they went over to England to prepare for the wedding on the twenty-second.

Whenever thoughts of the little life in the future came to her, they caused her fresh anguish and she thrust them aside fiercely. She would not let herself admit them at all as the days went on. She stamped out weakness and made herself practical.

Her face was changing. It had become hard, and while there was sorrow, there was also a cynical look in her eyes.

Jack's relations had welcomed her warmly, even the crusty old cousin from whom he would inherit the title someday. As far as her life as Jack's wife went, there seemed to be no clouds ahead.

Mrs Greening had had the great pleasure of collecting the bridesmaids—all children, they had decided, because Molly had two small daughters, of five and six, and "the Ladies Margaret and Ursula Brooklyn" would sound so well in the descriptions in the papers! beside the minute Earl of three, Molly's son and heir, as one of the pages.

Jack's titled relatives provided the other four girls and the other little page boy.

All these details had been of the greatest happiness to arrange, for Mrs Greening. Laline had assented to everything with a wan smile which had a sardonic curl in it, and once or twice she had laughed aloud, bitterly, alone in her room, at the grim mockery of it all.

"I need not wear orange blossoms, Auntie, need I?" she said. "I hate them, silly emblems of bygone days! I am going to have no wreath and no flowers, just the diamond bandeau the old Earl has given me, to keep the veil on, and the string of Jack's pearls."

"Why, you'll set a new fashion, Laline!" her Aunt exclaimed. "Modern girls have no sentiments like they used to have."

"Perhaps they have had the romance burnt out of them," her niece replied, and sighed. "And what is it anyway? Just a false glamour thrown over cruel facts."

Mrs Greening was horrified!

*   *   *

David reached a vantage point after his frantic gallop, and turning quickly wheeled to the left and disappeared behind a jutting angle of rock, and his pursuers thundered past him and soon were out of sight.

Then he encouraged his tired Arabian gently, and cantered on, taking a path at right angles, and soon was in safety in the friendly Chief's stronghold.

That had been a near shave! Nearer than when he had disposed of the two Greeks! But fighting and adventure were a delight to him really, and he rolled himself in his blanket and fell asleep in the moonlight, with a sense of exaltation in his heart.

In a few days more he would be in civilisation again, and then in Rome, for Laline's letter!

How glorious!

When he did reach the Grand Hotel in the Eternal City, his pulses were bounding with expectation and joy. What would she say, his darling!

Ah! Something divine, of course, since he knew that every throb of her heart beat love for him, and every thought of her spirit was filled with tenderness.

And then when they did meet! How they would rush into each other's arms! How they would talk and tell each other everything that had happened since they had parted, and then they would never, never part again.

Above all things, David was a practical person, not given to nervous questionings. He had made his decision that morning in Amiens, knowing his duty was to "carry the message to Garcia."

He had taken all precautions to ensure Laline's understanding of his motives, and not a disturbing doubt had ever entered his head since then.

When he had thought of her—which had been at every moment when his whole attention was not claimed by his work—it had always been with the fondest worship and trust, and he had made plans for their future and devised ways in which he could show her his devotion.

He almost bounded into the hall of the Grand Hotel, such was his eagerness.

There were no letters for Major Lamont!

The shock was great.

No letters at all! He had hardly expected any, except from Laline, unless Mr Randolph should have sent him fresh orders, since no one else knew that he would be in Rome.

Fergusson, of course, was waiting for him, but he had somehow missed him at the station, presuming that he had in fact gone to meet him.

He would go on up to the room which he found had been engaged for him, and he would see if there was anything there. If not, he would telephone to the Embassy.

But he had told Laline the Grand Hotel, in his letter, not the Embassy at all.

His heart had sunk now, and he felt extremely disturbed, for all the buoyant joyousness had fled.

No, there was nothing in his room. He went to the telephone.

It took some time to get on as usual, and he waited the few minutes with growing anxiety and distress.

At last he got the communication: no letters for Major Lamont at the Embassy.

He could easily catch the express for Paris that night.

It was only five o'clock, and he would be at the Gare de Lyon at six o'clock on the morning of the twenty-second of July, and when he had rushed to the Embassy to deliver the precious documents into Mr Randolph's hands, he would then be free to find Laline and discover what was the reason for her silence.

Should he telegraph to her at the Ritz? There would be no time for him to receive an answer before he started. No, that would be useless—better to get to her as fast as he could!

If she had not written, there was some reason for her silence. What reason? Had the exposure to cold and hunger caused her to be too ill to write?

This thought was a perfect agony. But it could not be that, because he had received assurances from Fergusson, before he left Amiens, that she was going on all right.

Starvation was not a disease, and the effects

of it wore off quickly with care and proper food, and Laline would have everything possible done for her.

Was she dead? Had some awful complication occurred? Oh, God! He could not face this! His anxiety now became almost unbearable. Had she never received his letter?

But of course she had. Lost letters occurred only in melodramas, not in real life. The chambermaid would have had no earthly reason not to deliver it, and even her Aunt and her faithful maid would not deliberately suppress correspondence, not in these days!

However, they might not have handed the letter to Laline immediately if it had fallen into their hands, Laline being asleep when the chambermaid went in.

Fergusson entered the room just then and they greeted each other. The servant was nettled at not meeting his master at the train.

David asked—demanded—eagerly if anything had come for him.

Nothing, Fergusson said.

Then he asked what news had been in the papers lately. Had he heard anything of the party they had left at Amiens?

But Fergusson had been away, "getting a bit of sport" with an American-Italian friend of his, and he had not seen any papers for a matter of three weeks.

There was nothing about them before that, except the *New York Herald* had said that Miss Lester and her Aunt had gone to England from the Ritz Hotel in Paris.

So Laline was not dead, nor even ill, then. What could it be?

Had she ceased to love him?

But this was perfectly ridiculous. Of course she had not. She loved him as he loved her, utterly and for eternity.

No, the probable thing, considering the strike that had been on in Italy, and the disorganisation of traffic, was that her letter to him had been lost.

But she would know that he would return to her on the instant he could, so he must not let himself speculate further, but must just wait patiently until he reached Paris and could make all investigations.

And so at last he boarded the train.

Chapter
Nine

It was raining on the morning of the twenty-second of July when Laline woke. But the sun came out afterwards, before her breakfast was brought up.

She was feeling ill and unutterably depressed. Celestine had been so troubled about her on the night before that she had given her a sleeping draught.

How was she going to get through the day? Her wedding day!

She could not prevent her thoughts from going to that other wedding of hers, there in the dug-out.

With what different feelings she had contemplated making the vows then, with death staring them in the face, and the probability of only a few hours, or days at best, with her beloved one.

She seemed to experience again all the thrills of exaltation, and to see David's face, filled with passionate love, bending over her.

Surely the present was some horrible dream, and she would awaken and find that he had returned to save her!

And what would the future be, if she went through with this ghastly mockery? Jack would go on being devoted, she could be sure of that, and she would have an honourable name and a place in the world. And there would be no scandal.

She was not deceiving Jack, or trying to thrust a cheat upon him. He was marrying her with his eyes open to everything but the ceremony of the marriage, and was that really a ceremony?

Here the everlasting question assailed her again. Was she doing something very wrong?

If David had simply disappeared, and there had been no trace of him after she had left Amiens, she would have waited and hoped, and even trusted him.

But it was the going off with Mrs Hamilton which made the thing so terrible ... so impossible to make excuses for ... so heartless ... so brutal.

He had deliberately deserted her, evidently to fulfil a plan he must have made before he ever went to the battlefields. This proved that his whole conduct towards her was false, a lie.

Now she began to reason that he could never have loved her. Only, she reflected bitterly, men could love two women at the same time!

He had always treated her with want of respect from the very beginning. From the kiss on the *Olympic* to the kiss in the car, always insolent until they were married. Here she clenched her hands in anger and pain.

No, she had a right to consider the ceremony as nothing, since he had shown her the way. But what if she met him someday in the future when she was Jack's wife ... ?

Celestine came in then with her breakfast, and understood by the look she saw in her mistress's face that it would be unwise to leave her alone again until she was ready to go to the Chapel.

Lady Molly Fordebrooke and her children had arrived the evening before. The house was crammed with guests, filled to its full capacity. There was an air of bustle and gaiety.

Through the open windows Laline could hear the birds singing, and the sound of the gardeners as they went in and out of the Chapel to put the finishing touches to the flowers.

Celestine said something joyous and cheerful. A final present from Jack lay upon the breakfast tray.

Everyone seemed to be rejoicing, except the bride.

"Celli ... the whole thing is impossible!" Laline said with a gasp. "I can't ... I can't go through with it!"

Then the maid because furious.

This was quite too bad, and not like her own *Mademoiselle*, or even a lady, to make a scandal and cause unhappiness to so great a *gentilhomme* as *le Capitaine* Lumley!

He, who had loved her always, who was now ready to give her the greatest honour in the world!

How could *Mademoiselle* even contemplate being so selfish as to break his heart? If he, knowing everything, was yet willing, and even more than eager, to make *Mademoiselle* his wife, whose business was it to create difficulties?

"That is just it, Celli. He does *not* know everything. He does not know about the priest having performed a ceremony." Laline's voice was despairing again.

This made Celestine uncomfortable. She

could not bear to remember that, about the priest, but whether or not, there was no use in bringing it up now.

One must be practical, and as *Monsieur le Major* would certainly deny any wedding, what would be the good of *Mademoiselle* remembering it?

Then Molly, in a dressing-gown, knocked at the door and came in, and seated herself on the bed.

"You do look woebegone, Laline!" she exclaimed. "What is the matter, dearest? You ought to be the happiest girl in the world."

"Of course I am."

"Then cheer up, for goodness' sake, or you will not look well in that perfect gown. Silver and gold! How right you were not to have plain white, or just silver, as everyone has now."

"Yes; I thought gold would be more suitable to me," Laline answered, and wondered if any of the ironical emotion she was feeling had crept into her voice.

Somehow, having Molly there, talking about clothes, seemed to make things more everyday and human, and not so awful to contemplate.

"Now do open your present, honey," Molly said, catching sight of the box on the tray.

She opened the parcel.

It had just "With Jack's Fond Love" on a card, and there she found a heart made of one large ruby, a quaint, unusual jewel of great price.

Dear Jack! She would wear it presently. The children came back with their mother, and brought her their little gifts, and then Mrs Greening arrived, and the chatter was incessant until past twelve o'clock.

There was no time for any more thinking or

grieving; Laline must get up and dress, and eat her luncheon, and have her hair done and her veil put on.

The ceremony was to be at half-past two, exactly. And a Bishop uncle of Jack's would give the blessing.

*　　*　　*

David arrived at the Gare de Lyon at about half-past six in the morning. It was raining in Paris, too. He had slept very little both nights on the train, and as he neared the station his anxiety and impatience seemed to have reached an unbearable pitch.

He got into a taxi as quickly as he could and drove straight to the American Embassy, half-an-hour's drive away. Even in this disturbed moment of his life, his duty came first with him.

The Ambassador was not yet up, but would put on a dressing-gown and come to him immediately, he was told, and he waited in the well-remembered sitting-room for ten or fifteen minutes.

Then Mr Randolph came in.

"Welcome back, Major Lamont!" he cried gladly, shaking his hand warmly. "You really have come up to time splendidly. Now, tell me all about it, boy."

So David gave up the precious documents, and the two sat down, and for more than an hour and a half David made his report and gave a detailed account of things, while the Ambassador listened attentively, asking many questions and taking down some notes.

"You had some narrow escapes," he said at last. "Well, it is a glorious thing to be young and to be able to see life, and you have earned the respect and grateful thanks of the Ministers who entrusted you with this important matter. You will not go unrewarded for this, Lamont, I can tell you."

"I was not thinking about reward, sir. I am proud to serve my country." And David lifted his head.

Then he thought he might now, perhaps, speak of his own affairs. So he turned the conversation to Mrs Randolph and asked how she was, and from that remarked:

"You remember Mrs Greening and her niece, Miss Lester, don't you, sir? Have you heard any news of them lately? I seem to have been away for an eternity, and of course have had no news of any of my friends."

His Excellency was looking down at his notes, and not paying much attention for the moment. He answered a little absently:

"Oh, the girl who was buried in the dug-out with you. Let me see. Yes! Isn't she going to be married soon to an Englishman? I think Mrs Randolph said something about it only yesterday.

"If I remember rightly, Lumley was the name. By the way, where did you say you believed the troop went on to after you doubled back and gave them the slip?"

David caught his breath for a second and then instantly controlled himself, telling the Ambassador of the place, and the rest of the information he required.

Then, when he had completely mastered all show of emotion, he asked:

"Do you happen to know where Mrs Greening and her niece are now, sir? Captain Lumley is a great friend of mine."

"I know that they went to England, but I do

not know where. They were here dining about three weeks ago."

David's one desire now was to get away, to be able to think. The frightful shock he had received had made him very pale. The Ambassador noticed it.

"I expect you are pretty tired, Lamont, after all your exertions, and are wanting a bath and breakfast. Well, I will not keep you any longer now. I can't tell you how I appreciate your splendid service. I'll telephone you in a day or two when I have heard from Washington. You'll be at the Ritz, as usual, I suppose?"

David said he would be, and so they shook hands again cordially and he made his way down the stairs, and as he passed the large buhl clock in the hall it chimed quarter-past nine.

He felt almost as though he was staggering when he got outside. The taxi was still waiting.

"To the Ritz!" he said to the driver quite fiercely.

What could this mean? Laline going to marry Jack Lumley, his friend Jack?

But how could she marry anyone? She was married already to him! She was his wife, his very own!

He pressed his hands to his head. Was he mad, or dreaming?

Then he remembered that the priest was dead and that there was no proof whatsoever of their wedding.

If Laline had forgotten him and their love sufficiently to be willing to marry Jack, it must mean that she *intended* to deny the ceremony. There would be only his word against hers.

What frightful thing had happened in the two months to change his darling? Whose influence had accomplished this? There would be a letter for him at the Ritz, most probably.

Certainly from Jack if not from Laline. People's characters could not completely alter from one month to another, and Jack's character was above reproof.

He would never marry Laline or in any way betray a trust to him if he knew the circumstances. Thus, it followed that Laline must have utterly deceived him.

Of course, there was no letter for him at the Ritz.

He went to his room, stunned. Then he plunged into a bath and tried to think.

When he came out of the bathroom, his breakfast had arrived and with it the papers.

He had come to the conclusion that he would telegraph to Jack at his club.

He opened the *Continental Daily Mail* and there saw a paragraph which sent the blood coursing furiously in his veins.

It was to the effect that the marriage of Captain Jack Lumley, cousin of the Earl of Channings, and Miss Laline Lester, the beautiful niece of Mrs Greening, of Washington, would take place in the Chapel at Channings Priory, Dover, at half-past two today, the 22nd of July!

Then followed the description of the bridesmaids and the guests who would be there.

For one moment David's hands seemed nerveless and he almost dropped the paper, then his strength of purpose reasserted itself. He was not of a character to accept fate resignedly.

He would fight to the last breath of life for what he considered to be truly his own.

He pulled himself together, and used all his wits.

The wedding was to be at half-past two. It was now ten; he had four and a half hours. He was in Paris, and the ceremony would be twenty miles inland from Dover.

Telegrams would be of no use. If they had gone as far as this, what attention would they pay to telegrams, even if he could be certain one would reach them?

Things were not yet at pre-war efficiency, and a wire was quite capable of taking four hours, and people did not open wires on wedding days, for they would receive dozens of congratulations.

It was no use chancing that. He would send one anyway, but the imperative necessity was that he should get there himself, in time.

He controlled all his nerves, and wrote out the telegram to Jack, addressing it "Channings Priory, Dover."

Then he called Fergusson, who had gone into the bathroom when his master came out, and was arranging his things.

"I have to be in England, Fergusson, before a quarter-past two. Telegraph to the Lord Warden at Dover for a car to meet me on the cliffs at the landing place for aeroplanes, while I telephone to the Military Attaché at the Embassy to find out the quickest way I can get a machine."

His voice was so quiet that Fergusson realised there was something very grave afoot. He knew his master well. He also was a person who could "carry a message to Garcia."

He did not stop to say "Would not some other conveyance do?" or make any other suggestions, he merely remarked, "Very good, sir," and immediately proceeded to carry out his master's orders, going into the hall to execute them.

After nearly half-an-hour's telephoning, David arranged that he should start from Buc at half-past eleven.

Fergusson returned now, having despatched his wire, which he had worded so that the urgency of the order for a car might be understood.

Then David, who had been hastily shaving and dressing between his telephone calls, was ready to start.

The only relic of Laline he possessed was her great sapphire ring, which had caught in the lining of his coat pocket, and had only been found when Fergusson had been drying the coat late that first night at Amiens, and which he had handed to his master on their journey to Paris.

"If there is a ring used today, it shall be this ring," David said with clenched teeth.

Then he went round to the office in the Rue des Petit Champs and sent his telegram himself to Jack, and a few minutes after eleven he was tearing out to Buc, in a Ritz car, with Fergusson beside him.

*   *   *

Laline finished the first part of her dressing and waited in a rose-coloured silk peignoir for the *coiffeur* to come and do her hair.

Molly had returned to the room, and was keeping up her spirits. The astute creature guessed that her school friend, for some perfectly incomprehensible reason, was not looking forward to her wedding with the joy she certainly should be experiencing.

Molly guessed the reason must be sentimental. What perfect nonsense!

Here Laline was going to marry into what she now termed her "rank in life," and her bridegroom was one of the nicest, dearest, most perfect gentlemen anyone could find, and he adored her, and would let her do exactly what she pleased afterwards.

And yet the tiresome girl was looking as glum as an owl, and Molly could see that she was almost on the edge of tears!

At last Celestine announced the *coiffeur*, and Molly left to finish her own dressing.

Jack, at the Lord Warden Hotel, in Dover, with his best man, was dressing too.

He was in a quiet state of mind. There was no anxiety in his heart. He knew *everything*, he felt, and so could start his life with Laline as his wife, unshadowed by possible surprises.

Love for him meant more than family or name or race.

Laline's child would be very dear to him, and perhaps someday he would have one of his own.

He tied his pale grey tie firmly, and then went down and ate a simple luncheon with his best man in the restaurant.

Celestine was beginning to feel terrible twinges. Long ago, before she had gone to America, she had been a Catholic, and even if religion had lapsed a good deal in the last ten years, somewhere in the back of her mind she was superstitious about it.

What if she had been influencing her lamb to commit a great sin? But then what will you? *Le Bon Dieu* was after all a gentleman, and would understand that the situation must be saved, and that it was extremely ill-bred, and *pas bon ton*, to make scandals.

There was nothing for it, nothing for it, but she wished it could have been otherwise!

Judge Whitmore was to give the bride away,

being so old a friend, and no male relation being present.

And Laline, as the time went on and she was left alone, with the *coiffeur* gone and her hair finished, to eat her chicken and drink a glass of milk, could do nothing but repeat a prayer, a prayer to ask for forgiveness, if she was going to commit a sin, and for strength to be able to make Jack happy.

For herself, life was over. Henceforth, her years must be devoted to trying to repay Jack's noble devotion.

It was too late now, she could not go back or change her mind.

They had all left her alone for the half-hour to eat her simple lunch, but now Molly burst in. She was going to help Celestine to clothe her in the marvellous gold-and-silver brocade bridal-dress, and fix her veil to flow beneath Jack's old cousin's diamond bandeau.

Celestine was unusually quiet and seemed once or twice to be brushing tears from her eyes, but Laline now was quite calm.

At last she was dressed, and a more beautiful bride never walked up to an altar.

The entirely plain, mediaeval-looking robe showed off her slender figure to perfection, its long sleeves coming over her almost transparent little hands. Round her bare neck, on a long slender diamond chain, hung Jack's ruby heart.

Her plain tulle veil fell from the diamond bandeau over the silver-cloth train lined with gold, which hung from her shoulders.

Laline herself was as pale as a white rose, and her eyes were cast down, the curly golden-brown lashes resting on blue shadows.

A mystic bride from some fifteenth-century

stained-glass Church window come to life, she appeared, not a real modern young woman.

"You are just too divine!" Molly said.

The little bridesmaids and pages were all collected now in the great hall, with anxious attendants giving them last instructions.

Mrs Greening was waiting, bouquet in hand, and the guests who had come by train and motor were beginning to drift into the Chapel, where the clergymen had already gone.

The sun shone, the birds sang, and the great clock had already, several minutes ago, chimed quarter-past two.

Laline was to carry an ivory-bound prayerbook, not the usual bouquet, and at the last moment it could not be found.

Molly had unwrapped it from its packing and laid it down somewhere, but where? She and Celestine began to lose their heads about it. The bride stood in her oak-panelled bed-room, apparently perfectly calm.

Was she frozen to stone? This was not Laline, not the Laline who had married her love in the face of death, in an underground excavation, clothed in a blue silk jersey frock, just over two months before; this white-faced, stately, golden-robed bride was not Laline.

She clasped her hands together for a second to feel if she was real, the same impulse which used to make her touch the bristles on David's chin, when hunger and privation were beginning to make things shadowy to her.

Yes, she was real, just as he had been. But why did she seem to be seeing his eyes all the time, looking at her out of the dark panelling? Eyes so full of reproach and sorrow, not fierce and passionate as his eyes so often were.

Oh, would Molly and Celestine never find the prayer-book? Better to start and get the frightful sacrilege over. She could not bear this waiting. She would begin to scream.

The distracted maid discovered it at last, hidden under a black lace scarf which Mrs Greening had dropped on a table the last time she had bustled into the room.

Celestine took this for an omen, and nearly let the book fall as she handed it to her mistress.

Hidden under a black cloud, the blessing of God! But what was to be done?

"Run to the minstrels'-gallery and peep and see if they've all gone on but the bridesmaids and pages, and Judge Whitmore," Molly said, and Celestine went.

* * *

Jack arrived at the side door of the Chapel with his best man, a brother officer in the Guards Battalion in which they had both served.

They stayed by the vestry door beyond the huge banks of flowers.

The clergymen had moved into place. The organ was playing soft music. The guests were seated, and now the bride's Aunt, the house party, and all Jack's relations came in and took their seats, and there was that air of expectancy and that feeling of excitement which there always is at weddings.

Jack's heart began to beat and the best man coughed and muttered.

"Buck up, old chap."

Then half-past two chimed from the clock tower.

* * *

David arrived in plenty of time at Buc, but there was nearly half-an-hour's delay before the aeroplane could start.

He fumed inwardly, but the wind seemed all right, and surely it could not take two hours to get over the Channel and land on the cliffs at Dover.

If the motor was there waiting, they could do the twenty miles in twenty minutes and he would be able to prevent the ceremony.

Each time his thoughts reached this point, a wild anger shook him. How had they dared to contemplate committing such an action as to get married?

Supposing he did not reach there before half-past two, and the ceremony was finished; in the eyes of the law, Laline would be Jack's wife, not his, since the priest was dead and there had been no witnesses.

The time he had to wait for the aeroplane to start was the worst he had yet gone through in his life.

But at last he was high up in the sky, among the clouds, which were clearing away, and an hour later he could see the blue sea beneath him.

He now began to speculate more reasonably as to what could have happened.

It was unlikely that Laline had utterly ceased to love him because he had gone away. His letter to her had explained everything quite satisfactorily, and surely she could trust him.

Could she somehow have heard that Mrs Hamilton had been on the train, and she had been confoundedly jealous?

Laline had always shown signs of being jealous of the Ambassador's niece, but that would be ridiculous, since she knew perfectly well that he adored her, and the other woman was a mere acquaintance.

He had perhaps been stupid ever to tease her; he now remembered that he had not given her any satisfactory answer on the subject in the dug-out when they both were in a playful mood.

But even so, his having chanced to be on the train with the woman could not be enough cause to make Laline want to ruin all their future happiness in this awful manner.

Could family pressure have been put upon her? He did not know Mrs Greening well, and perhaps she had more authority over his darling girl than she appeared to have.

But, Jack's part! That was the most incomprehensible of all, since he had told Laline to tell Jack everything, as the one safe person to confide in.

David sifted each possible aspect of the affair as he crossed the Channel, and before they reached the cliffs he had come to a conclusion which was near the truth.

If by some diabolical turn of fate Laline had never received his letter, and imagined he had deserted her, and someone had seen him leave the Ritz with Mrs Hamilton and gossipped to her about it, jealousy and the belief believing that he was a scoundrel might have driven her to take Jack, out of pique.

Pique? No, that was not a sufficiently strong motive after a love like theirs. Laline had shown him that her character was of pure gold.

No matter how piqued she might have felt, she would have allowed some time to pass, and given him a chance to come back and explain.

Could it be—was it that she *had to marry someone?* Could it be that, believing she had been deliberately abandoned by him, she had accepted Jack?

"Oh! Good God!" David gasped aloud, and quite startled Fergusson.

Yes, this must be the explanation, it was the only one which could account for things. Jack, of course, would have come up to the scratch like the splendid friend he always was, unless Laline had deceived him, which was unlikely.

From now onwards, David's thoughts became a nightmare of anxiety.

He *must* reach Channings Priory before half-past two.

A rather ramshackle-looking old car was waiting when at last they landed safely, and giving Fergusson instructions to make his way to the Lord Warden in Dover and stay there until he received further instructions, David got into the car.

The driver explained that there was a tremendous rush of tourists just now, and that on such short notice this was the only car available.

"But she'll get you to the wedding in time, sir, all right. I suppose it's the wedding at the Priory you're going to?"

David nodded but remained silent. His heart was beating as if in his throat, for his watch said that it was quarter to two, and this rotten car could never make more than twenty miles an hour.

He felt that he would like to get out and push it as they went on!

It would appear sometimes that anxious thoughts delay events, for just as they came at last to the paddocks, and could see the chimneys of the house in the distance, with groans and creakings the old motor came to a standstill.

A wild passion of rage and despair shook David.

What was to be done? How could he reach the Chapel? It was now five minutes to the half-hour.

He gazed round frantically. If he ran with all his strength, he could not cover the distance, and climb the probable fences, in time.

Then a gentle whinny caught his ear, and he saw the beautiful eyes of a thoroughbred gazing at him over the top of a tall iron gate, which he could see was padlocked.

There were other horses grazing farther in. Here was the desperate last chance. He did not hesitate for even an instant. Fortunately, he knew all about horses and their ways.

He climbed the gate very quietly, so as not to frighten the creature, and then, luck aiding him, he caught its stable halter and leapt onto its bare back, and was off like a nomad.

"Steady, girl, steady," he kept murmuring, and guided the animal towards where the house seemed to be.

The hedge which divided the paddocks from the park was not a very high one. The clock in the tower at that moment chimed half-past two. This maddened David, and with a wild cry he put the mare at the hedge, while he bent and clung to her mane.

The beautiful creature answered to his knee movements and took the hedge at a flying leap, but stumbled a little a few paces afterwards, and David nearly lost his seat; but, righting himself, he galloped forward.

He must be, *must be*, in time!

* * *

Celestine returned from the minstrels'-gallery to say that everyone had gone on but Judge Whitmore and the bridesmaids and pages.

So, Laline and Molly left the room, and, followed by the maid who was carrying the train, they went down the great stairs to the hall.

Molly kissed Laline, who was now as white as death.

"Why, you are too beautiful, darling! You must keep up your courage," she whispered.

The procession started then, Laline leaning on Judge Whitmore's arm.

There was a murmur of admiration from the onlookers as the procession swept through the cloisters; and indeed, a more lovely bride had never been seen.

"Silver and gold and white!" as one of the farmers' wives whispered romantically. "For her face is as white as her veil, and her hair is as gold as her dress. Isn't she perfect!"

"Won't Captain Jack be happy!" another exclaimed ecstatically.

The Chapel door was reached and the train disappeared within, while the organ played sympathetically.

Jack moved forward to meet his bride, and Molly, passing the bridesmaids, reached her place beside Mrs Greening in the front pew.

The music ceased, and after an instant's silence the clergyman began the opening words of the service.

Laline now was hardly conscious of anything. She heard vaguely the sound of the solemn words, but did not take in the full meaning, only they seemed something terrible and menacing.

She knew that she must stand up straight presently and repeat what she was told.

But oh! if only the beam of blue light, which was coming from a southern stained-glass window high up, could enter her heart and take away her life, how much better that would be.

God was angry with her, and she would be cursed, not blessed.

Wild thoughts came. Should she scream and say she could not go through with it?

David . . . David! Her darling, her real husband. Where was he?

But what was that noise of galloping horse's hoofs on the stones of the cloisters? There was then a confused murmur of voices outside, heard above the quiet tones of the officiating priest.

This was unseemly, so he spoke more loudly.

"Therefore, if any man can show any just cause why they may not be joined together, let him now speak, or else hereafter forever hold his peace."

Chapter
Ten

David galloped forward at breakneck pace, straight for the Chapel, which, he could now see, was in the garden. And as he came nearer he could see the bridal procession leaving the house.

The sound of the horse's hoofs were not heard on the soft turf, nor did anyone realise that a wild horseman was advancing. The tenants' backs were turned from the park, and all eyes were fixed on the bride.

It was only when the bare-backed rider, without hat now, and clad in a grey flannel suit, entered the cloisters, and clattered along the flag-stones at the side of the red carpet, that the crowd were startled violently, and some of the women shrieked.

David was like young Lochinvar, nothing stopped him, and he flung himself off the mare so rapidly that no one could hinder him, at the very door of the Chapel, which he entered with great strides.

The animal when left alone reared, and a gardener caught it and led it, all covered with foam, away to the stable yard.

Then the onlookers surged forward to get as near the door as possible, to witness what all felt would soon be a drama taking place.

It was when the words "or else hereafter forever hold his peace" were being said, that David dashed up the aisle, passing the frightened little bridesmaids, his eyes flashing and his face pale.

"I forbid this marriage to go on," he said in a firm, strong voice as he reached the chancel steps. "I know cause and just impediment why it should not take place."

The guests in the seats were craning their heads with excitement, and the smallest page began to cry. All became confusion.

But Laline knew nothing of it, for when she had heard David's voice, which had seemed to come to her through space, she had given a cry and fallen forward, unconscious, and had been clasped in Jack's fond arms.

The nurses and governesses, in the back pews, had the good sense to go at once to each of their charges, and the little children were rapidly led away, back to the house.

Mrs Greening and Molly rushed to Laline's side, and while Molly rubbed the nerveless white hand which hung limp, Mrs Greening turned on David, who stood there towering above her like a bronze statue, so still was he.

"How dare you make this disturbance, Major Lamont!" the infuriated Aunt almost screamed.

The Bishop who was to have delivered the blessing now stepped forward.

"Let all the congregation leave this House of God," he said, raising his old, thin hand. "And let this man who has broken in upon us have his say."

The guests made way for Jack now to carry

Laline down the aisle and so on through the cloisters to the hall.

The head gardener, with the good taste of an old servant, had marshalled the tenants to a distance off, and they were dispersing; so the way was clear, and Jack never stopped until he had laid the unconscious girl on the bed in her own room, Molly following him.

Celestine had gone back there from the hall; at the last moment her courage had failed her, and she could not witness the ceremony, which she now felt to be a crime.

She had heard the disturbance and noise of the horse's hoofs, and was holding her hand to her heart when Jack, carrying his precious burden, entered the room.

"Mon adorée! My lamb!" she cried despairingly. "What has happened?" And she went at once to her beloved mistress's side.

"Get the salts," Molly commanded firmly, for she did not lose her head.

"Is she dead?" asked Jack in a frozen voice; it was the first word he had spoken.

They cared for the poor child tenderly, and in a few minutes she opened her eyes, then Jack left them and went back to the Chapel.

David and the clergymen were just coming out through the door when Jack met them, and the two whilom friends glared at each other face to face.

"You must answer to me now, you scoundrel," Jack said sternly.

But the Bishop intervened.

"Let there be no angry words before you have heard each other," he implored.

So Jack and David walked back again into

the house, and to the library, and when they had entered Jack shut the door.

"Laline is my wife," David said in a grave, quiet voice. "The priest married us in the dug-out before he died."

"You are lying," Jack hurled at him. "If it had been so, she would have told me."

David stepped back a pace and put his hand to his head.

"There was no proof of the marriage, only our words, and Laline may have thought I would deny it on my side."

"Oh my God!" cried Jack in anguish, light breaking in upon him. "Go on!"

"I wrote her a letter at Amiens that morning, explaining that I had to go immediately for two months, on service for our country, and could give no account of myself until the end of that time.

"I asked her to trust me, and to tell no one but you of the wedding, because it was of the utmost importance that no talk should centre round my name, until my mission was accomplished."

He paused.

"You surely understand, knowing my work in the war. I conclude she never received that letter. I gave it to the chambermaid to hand to her personally as soon as she should be awake. I had not one minute to lose, for I had to be at the Embassy at twelve o'clock at the end of my six days' leave.

"It was pretty ghastly, having to go, but there was nothing for it, and I knew she'd trust me when she understood. Jack, is it that she did not get the letter at all?"

All the life seemed to die out of Jack's face as he listened; now he looked up, though, with his honest blue eyes.

"No, she never received it. She thought you had deliberately deserted her, and gone to Rome with another woman. The evidence we heard at the Ritz was absolutely incontrovertible. How do you account for that?"

His tone hardened, and again he glared fiercely at his old friend.

David did not become angry. The whole thing was growing clear to him now, and great sorrow for the pain his comrade would have to suffer was in his heart.

"I did not know anything about the confounded woman's going, until the Ambassador asked me to take care of her, she being his niece, and because the Italian railway strike was on. I had only seen her once before in my life, and of course I left her as soon as we reached Rome."

Jack sank into a chair and supported his head in his hands.

"It is all too awful," he said. "If you knew the cruel unhappiness Laline has been through, and then, at last, it seemed that you had deliberately betrayed and abandoned her, and so I . . ."

David held out his hand.

"Jack, you splendid chap," he cried brokenly, "you asked her to marry you to save the situation, was that not it? I understand."

David was so deeply moved that his voice was hoarse with emotion. Jack looked up now.

"I asked her to marry me because I love and honour her more than anyone on earth. I have been asking her continually ever since we first

met, and now, above all, for I knew that she
needed protection and care."

A reverence filled David. This was love indeed; he himself could not have done that.

"You always said love was devotion, Jack
old man, and I said it was action. I could not
have made such a sacrifice, and because of love
for a woman given my name to another man's
child. You are far beyond me—I—I . . ."

His voice broke and he could not go on.
Jack straightened himself.

"The only thing we have to consider now is
Laline's happiness."

David walked to the window and spoke with
his back turned.

"Jack, you are far more worthy of her than
I am. Has she grown to know it, and to love
you? Because if so, I'll go away now. There is
no proof of our wedding, she knew that, and of
course I can see that she, thinking I would deny
it, never even told you.

"We can say this fuss has all been a mistake.
I did not tell the parsons anything, only that I
must speak to you alone."

He paused. Jack did not speak, so he went
on:

"Jack old man, tell me the truth, and if it is
that she loves you, I'll crush everything out of
my heart and go at once."

For one awful moment Jack was tempted, for
he knew David would accept his word and not
even ask for further proof. But the temptation
passed, and he rose to his feet and went over to
his old friend.

"I could not lie like that, David; even if I
thought that now, having seen you again, Laline

would go through with it, I could not be such a mean sneak. I know she cares only for you and never has cared for me."

They wrung each other's hands silently, and then Jack said:

"Come."

Up in the oak-panelled bed-room, Laline was lying on the sofa. Celestine had taken off her wedding-robe and wrapped her in a white dressing-gown.

When she had recovered consciousness, her one thought was to get Molly to leave her alone with her maid. Celestine guessed this, and had tactfully manoeuvred Lady Fordebrooke from the room.

Then Laline held out her arms to her Celli.

"Tell me, tell me . . . was it really he?" she whispered wildly. "Oh, why does he not come to me now?"

At that moment the door opened and Jack came first, and David followed him up to the sofa.

Laline sprang to her feet.

"Laline," Jack said, his brave voice very deep. "It's all a mistake about David's going away on purpose. He'll tell you everything, dear."

And then as the lovers, with wild cries of joy, rushed into each other's arms, Jack beckoned Celestine, and they both turned and left them alone in the room.

* * *

Joy is the greatest reviver there is in the world, and Laline's pale face was glowing and radiant as she nestled in David's fond arms half-an-hour later, when the whole thing had been explained.

"But I shall always hate Mrs Hamilton," she

whispered, with true female rancour. "It is she, and not you, David, who made me suffer so!"

Every little point was gone into, and then they had their perfectly divine knowledge to talk over in whispers, and make plans for their future.

To avoid all scandal and chattering, they would say nothing of the ceremony in the dug-out, because it might cast a reflection upon Laline's having consented to become Jack's wife.

They would just be married over again, as soon as a licence could be procured, and all the civil rites attended to, and then they would go right away in blessed joy together, never to part again.

"Auntie will be perfectly furious that I am not someday going to be a Countess, and everyone will talk their heads off. But do we care?" Laline laughed.

"I care for nothing but you, darling," David said passionately.

"And you understand and have forgiven me for deciding to marry Jack?" she asked, and rubbed her soft cheek against his dark face in her old way.

"I understand everything," he said, and he held her to him. "The only shadow upon our happiness, my darling, is the thought of that dear old chap."

"Isn't he the most splendid, true gentleman on earth, David! When I think of him I could cry."

"Darling, I'll try to love you with the same marvellous devotion that old Jack does, but my nature is different—I am always rather wild."

"I should think you are!" Laline laughed softly in pride. "Imagine coming in an aeroplane, and riding one of the old man's thoroughbreds,

bare-backed, just to stop me from becoming someone else's! Oh, David, I just adore you! That's
all!"

*   *   *

And so, presently, they were married properly in London, and Judge Whitmore again gave the
bride away.

It was the quietest possible wedding, from
Molly's house in Grosvenor Square. Mrs Greening
was too incensed to be present.

If her niece liked to make such a fool of herself, she washed her hands of the whole affair!

But the lovers were off down to a Devonshire Manor House to stay for the summer in
delicious, happy peace.

"Darling, my own love!" David whispered
that night as they stood on the terrace in the
moonlight, overlooking the sea. "I never believed
that I could ever really love any woman, but you
are my heart and body and soul!"

And away upon the deck of a yacht that
was steaming down Channel, Jack was gazing at
the swirling green waters which curled away from
the bow.

The girl he worshipped was happy now.

That was the glorious thing, and someday,
when the stupid outside pain had lessened a bit,
he would come back and see her again; and perhaps in the future, the child which he had been
going to call his would give him its little affection
and they would be pals.

And because of this thought, which was always with him, his sad heart grew comforted.

But the two in the Devonshire garden were
beyond thinking of anything but their own two

selves, and their unutterable bliss. Everything else for them had melted into nothingness.

For they had found the only thing which is really worth finding in this old world:

True Love.

ABOUT THE EDITOR

BARBARA CARTLAND, the world's most famous romantic novelist, who is also an historian, playwright, lecturer, political speaker and television personality, has now written over 200 books. She has also had many historical works published and has written four autobiographies as well as the biographies of her mother and that of her brother Ronald Cartland, who was the first Member of Parliament to be killed in the last war. This book has a preface by Sir Winston Churchill. Barbara Cartland has sold 80 million books over the world, more than half of these in the U.S.A. She broke the world record in 1975 by writing twenty books in a year, and her own record in 1976 with twenty-one. In private life, Barbara Cartland, who is a Dame of the Order of St. John of Jerusalem, has fought for better conditions and salaries for Midwives and Nurses. As President of the Royal College of Midwives (Hertfordshire Branch), she has been invested with the first Badge of Office ever given in Great Britain, which was subscribed to by the Midwives themselves. She has also championed the cause for old people and founded the first Romany Gypsy Camp in the world. Barbara Cartland is deeply interested in Vitamin Therapy and is President of the British National Association for Health.

Introducing...
Barbara Cartland's
Library of Love

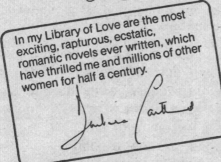

In my Library of Love are the most exciting, rapturous, ecstatic, romantic novels ever written, which have thrilled me and millions of other women for half a century.

Barbara Cartland

The World's Great Stories of Romance Specially Abridged by Barbara Cartland For Today's Readers.

Barbara Cartland

The world's bestselling author of romantic fiction. Her stories are always captivating tales of intrigue, adventure and love.

Barbara Cartland

The world's bestselling author of romantic fiction. Her stories are always captivating tales of intrigue, adventure and love.

☐	2107	A VERY NAUGHTY ANGEL	—$1.25
☐	2140	CALL OF THE HEART	—$1.25
☐	2147	AS EAGLES FLY	—$1.25
☐	2148	THE TEARS OF LOVE	—$1.25
☐	2149	THE DEVIL IN LOVE	—$1.25
☐	2436	THE ELUSIVE EARL	—$1.25
☐	2972	A DREAM FROM THE NIGHT	—$1.25
☐	10977	PUNISHMENT OF A VIXEN	—$1.50
☐	6387	THE PENNILESS PEER	—$1.25
☐	6431	LESSONS IN LOVE	—$1.25
☐	6435	THE DARING DECEPTION	—$1.25
☐	8103	CASTLE OF FEAR	—$1.25
☐	8240	THE RUTHLESS RAKE	—$1.25
☐	8280	THE DANGEROUS DANDY	—$1.25
☐	8467	THE WICKED MARQUIS	—$1.25
☐	11101	THE OUTRAGEOUS LADY	—$1.50
☐	11168	A TOUCH OF LOVE	—$1.50
☐	11169	THE DRAGON AND THE PEARL	—$1.50

Buy them at your local bookseller or use this handy coupon: